CHAPTER
ONE

Though no one would belittle the benevolence of the Good Samaritan, in one respect he was lucky: he was alone with his conscience and his neighbour in trouble.

There were, for instance, no business or professional colleagues to warn against the folly of interference; and no wife to cherish him for his altruism but also shrewdly to point out likely repercussions. Those voices Charles Forbes had to heed on the occasion when he, too, decided not to pass by on the other side.

The decision was made on a dull June day, near the end of term, as he sat at his desk in his schoolroom in the east end of Glasgow. The pupils in front of him were supposed to be writing a composition on "The Sea". Most of them were trifling. Outside in the street tramcars, lorries, motor-cars, rattled by. A pylon rose like a gigantic spider out of a garden of dandelions protected by barbed wire; and all around soared other fantastic growths, tall factory stacks, branchless, leafless, and blossomless.

On Mr Forbes's desk lay a grubby copy-book, and beside him stood its small thirteen-year-old owner, with his fingers intertwined behind his back.

Although it was fat, Mr Forbes's face was also long and bleak; even the little bags under his eyes were lugubrious. The result was that, despite his longing to be original in the display of compassion, all his grimaces were platitudes. His hand that rested on the blotted page was plump, soft, and pink, with black hairs and a ring; and his long look at the submissive blot-maker was so ambiguous that some of the other scholars, peeping up, thought he was about to explode into one of his homilies, so righteous and dull.

At last he spoke, in his most pontifical tones.

"Tell me, Curdie, have you ever seen the sea?"

Some of the class laughed. This was IA, the Latin scholars, the élite of the first year. Their parents had honoured their sons' brains by dressing them as well as limited means allowed. Most wore dark-blue crested blazers, clean shirts, flannel shorts, and the light-blue school tie. All were in contrast to this little scarecrow by the desk, in the ragged man's jacket, the filthy long trousers, and the sandshoes with the canvas tops in tatters. When he replied quietly, with no shame or even diffidence, that he had never really seen the sea and therefore his composition was just made up, they sneered at him like so many little Columbuses, with the marvels and avarice of oceans in their eyes. They were far from knowing that he had given that answer, which was a lie, because he knew that they, and the teacher, were greedy for it.

"I thought so, Tom," said Mr Forbes, with a heavy sigh. "But if you have not seen it, you have imagined it most beautifully."

The Changeling

With an afterword by Andrew Marr

ROBIN JENKINS

ISIS
LARGE PRINT
Oxford

Copyright © Robin Jenkins, 1958
Afterword Copyright © Andrew Marr, 2008

First published in Great Britain 1958
by
MacDonald & Co. (Publishers)

Published in Large Print 2009 by ISIS Publishing Ltd.,
7 Centremead, Osney Mead, Oxford OX2 0ES
by arrangement with
Canongate Books Ltd.

The moral right of the author has been asserted

British Library Cataloguing in Publication Data
Jenkins, Robin, 1912–2005.
The changeling
1. Problem youth - - Fiction.
2. Teacher-student relationships - - Fiction.
3. Glasgow (Scotland) - - Social conditions
- - Fiction.
4. Large type books.
I. Title
823.9'14–dc22

ISBN 978–0–7531–8374–8 (hb)
ISBN 978–0–7531–8375–5 (pb)

Printed and bound in Great Britain by
T. J. International Ltd., Padstow, Cornwall

With his leer of sympathy he contemplated this small, smiling, incommunicable, deprived morsel of humanity beside him. Curdie's smile was notorious: other teachers called it sly and insolent; it was, they said, the smile of the certificated delinquent, of misanthropy in bud, of future criminality, of inevitable degradation. Forbes refused to accept it as such; to him it indicated that this slum child, born so intelligent, was not only acknowledging the contempt and ridicule which his dress and his whole economic situation must incur, but was also making his own assessment of those who contemned and ridiculed. The result was not a vicious snarl, but this haunting courageous smile. It was possible, it was likely, that the boy would ultimately become debased. Who would not, born and bred in Donaldson's Court, one of the worst slums in one of the worst slum districts in Europe? There rats drank at kitchen sinks, drunkards jabbed at each other's faces with broken bottles, prostitutes carried on their business on stairheads, and policemen dreaded to enter. Most children brought up there were either depraved or protected by impenetrable stupidity.

Tom Curdie, on the contrary, had one of the best intelligences in the school. Properly fed, clothed, rested, and encouraged, he could go on to the University and have a brilliant career. As it was, malnourished, in rags, gnawed at daily by corrupting influences, discouraged everywhere, and perpetually tired through sleeping in a room with his brother and sister, where his mother and her horrible paramour also slept, he still could hold his own among the cleverest of his contemporaries, and could excel these in the strange beauty of his imagination.

It was true he had taken part in the burglary of a shop. His accomplices had stolen cigarettes and sweets, he packets of butter: that, which had amused others, had convinced Forbes, himself so well creashed, that bodily craving more than vice had impelled the child. Nevertheless, he had been brought to court, found guilty, and put on a year's probation. "You know what that means, Tom?" Forbes had asked sternly. "Yes, sir. It means if I do anything wrong in the next year I'd better no' be found out." Others would have interpreted that as impertinence, some would have punished him for it; but Forbes, accused so often of having no humour himself, saw the reply as a flash of sad but valiant irony. So much wrong had been done to this boy. By whom it had been done, Forbes could not quite say, except that he as a member of society must accept share of the blame. Hitherto he had seen no way by which to make amends. Now he saw a way.

Every year he and his family — Mary, his wife, and Alistair and Gillian, his children — spent their summer holiday at Towellan, a little village on the Firth of Clyde, two or three miles from the popular resort Dunroth. Those who thought meanness or economy was the reason for returning there summer after summer were ludicrously wrong. Towellan was not just a place where a holiday was spent, it was where the Forbes family renewed itself, where their love for one another, their faith, trust, and hope, were strengthened. Every pebble on the shore in front of the cottage, every leaf in the wood behind, every sprig of heather on the farther hills, were hallowed and possessed of this vitalising power. There, in his mauve corduroy shorts, Forbes might be laughed at by passing tourists, Mary, his sweet-blooded wife, sucked by clegs, and the two children tormented by ennui on wet afternoons, but always by the end of the month all four returned home tanned, happy, and invigorated in spirit as well as body.

So the idea came to Forbes. Why not take Tom Curdie with them this summer, not just to feed him and give him rest and fresh air, but especially to build up in him an immunity against the evil influences threatening him?

"Thalassa," murmured Forbes, as he made his vow, for in his time he had been one of Xenophon's men when they had caught sight of the sea after their long march, and now he would be with young Tom Curdie having his first experience of the beautiful Firth of Clyde.

The boy stood with his hands still behind his back. These queer noises and grimaces which the fat teacher was making were typical and funny, but amusement, like suffering, must never be shown.

The period bell rang. Hubbub of departure broke out.

"All right, Tom," said Forbes, dismissing him.

As the boy walked back to his place the dirt on his neck was more clearly seen; and were those red specks flea-marks? A voice whispered to Mr Forbes to cancel his vow. Where fleas were there might be lice; and if

5

Mary detested clegs and midges, she loathed fleas and lice.

"It would be cowardly," muttered Forbes, "to let lice defeat me."

There was, however, another obstacle: the headmaster's approval might not be necessary, but to so loyal and punctilious a subordinate as Forbes it was desirable.

With the copy-book in hand he went down to the head's room. Knocking, and waiting to allow Mr Fisher time to assume the appearance at least of managerial industry, he entered.

Mr Fisher, white-haired and affable, had been smoking a cigarette and dreaming of his forthcoming holiday on the Isle of Wight. When Forbes entered, however, he was crouched in his chair with his hands clasped, as if he was seeking by some kind of Yogi meditation to find a remedy for the shrinkage in children's brains which headmasters all over the country were lamenting. When he saw who his caller was he found it hard to dissemble his dismay. Forbes usually came with the most exasperating and inconsiderate requests. No other teacher was so optimistic in discovering children who ought to be promoted; he had no respect for the sanctity of the time-table.

Forbes made his customary little bow. Sometimes his chief thought it funny, sometimes pathetic, sometimes even dignified, but often insubordinate in the subtlest manner. Always it made him uncomfortable.

"I beg your pardon for interrupting you, Mr Fisher," said Forbes.

"Not a bit of it, Charlie. Sit down. What's on your mind?"

Forbes placed the copy-book on the desk in front of his chief. "Read that, Mr Fisher," he said.

Mr Fisher, groaning within at this inconvenient zeal, in June too, with the session's marks all tabulated, glanced over the composition. Himself in his day a teacher of mathematics, he had no feeling for style in literature. He wondered what he was expected to say. Was this some kind of trap?

"A bit grubby, isn't it?" he murmured.

"Let that pass. What of the matter?"

"Not bad, not bad at all."

"Mr Fisher, would you believe me if I were to tell you that the boy who wrote that has never seen the sea?"

The headmaster looked at the name on the outside. Immediately he bristled.

"So it's Curdie's?" he said. "What's he been up to this time? Miss Strang had him down yesterday. She caught him grinning insolently at her."

Forbes, too, grew stiff. It was his belief that Miss Strang, who taught French, had a spite against the boy because of his rags.

"I am not here to complain," he said.

"Thank goodness for that. I don't like strapping him. Pity's what he should get, but who could risk giving it to him?"

"I could, Mr Fisher. That boy lies under an Everest, a whole Himalayan range, of handicaps, disadvantages,

7

and penalties. Yet he has never revealed, to me at any rate, one whimper of complaint, one yelp for revenge."

"He's deep, Charlie, deep and sly."

"No, Mr Fisher. He is magnanimous."

"But, Charlie, he's a convicted thief."

"Magnanimity, Mr Fisher."

"A thick skin, more likely."

"But magnanimity, especially a child's, is exhaustible. When it is gone, ineradicable rancour must take its place."

Like an ingenuous pupil, the headmaster pretended bright interest. Inwardly he commiserated with himself on thus being bothered by this pompous bore who, it was said, had twice lost the chance of promotion because at both the interviews he had moralised thus to the councillors.

"I've come to the conclusion, Mr Fisher, that it isn't enough to draw my salary, and at four o'clock each day turn my back and retreat to my suburban sanctuary."

"I'm sure none of us do that, Charlie."

"I have done so. I speak only for myself. Here, as I see it, is my chance to atone. Mr Fisher, I propose to take Tom Curdie with my family to Towellan this summer. It seems to me the experience might give the boy some support in the battle which he has constantly to wage against corruption. I am here to seek your advice."

Faced with that vast, sanctimonious, aggressive pout, the headmaster grew peeved. Originality of most kinds he distrusted, but original goodness most of all.

"You want my honest opinion, Charlie?"

"Naturally."

"Then I'm telling you, emphatically, you'd be doing a very foolish thing. You'd ruin your holiday. You're mistaken about Curdie, you know. Bob Black of Oldlands Primary had him for seven years. He warned me particularly about him. And you know what Mr Todd thinks of him."

Todd, the deputy headmaster and principal maths teacher, thought Curdie was a practised liar and thief. He also thought all humanity was born wicked and had to be coerced into virtue.

"He thinks wee Curdie's the most dangerous boy in the school, Charlie, worse even than big Alboe."

Alboe was the school moron and bully. Periodically he had to be disarmed; now it would be a knife, now a razor blade on a stick, and now a lavatory chain with handle.

"You can see Alboe coming," said Mr Fisher, "but Curdie's sleekit and clever."

"Is it not possible his restraint may spring from courage?"

"Oh, he's no coward. I'll grant you that, Charlie. Have you considered it'd mean getting entangled with his family? You know what a proper hell's brew they're said to be. Donaldson's Court? If I'd a pet tiger I wouldn't let it go in yonder. What does your wife say?"

"I have not discussed it with her yet."

Mr Fisher laughed. "I see. It's just a notion that's floated into your head? She'll see that it floats out again."

"My wife is a very generous woman."

"Charlie, all our wives are, bless them."

"No." The simple negative was not enough; it had to be followed by a firm shake of the head: thus only Mrs Forbes among wives was generous. "If I was asked for an example of the indomitability of the human spirit, out of our whole school, Mr Fisher, I should choose little Tom Curdie."

Mr Fisher was overwhelmed. "Now, Charlie," he muttered, "don't lose sight of realities altogether. You'll tell Mrs Forbes he's been in the hands of the police?"

"She knows that. I have spoken to her about this boy often."

"I'll tell you what we could do. His character's against him, but maybe we could get him a fortnight at one of the Corporation's holiday homes."

"Institutional treatment is not what's wanted," said Forbes. "That would be a typical shirking of the problem. If there is to be salvation there must be sacrifice, and risk too, if you like. You raise no objection then?"

"How could I, Charlie? It's a private matter between you and Curdie's people."

"Thank you, Mr Fisher. I should be obliged if this remained confidential."

The headmaster accompanied him to the door.

"It's a generous impulse, Charlie," he said. "I'll say that for it. We all have them, you know. God, the number of unfortunate children I've wished to father in my time!" Too late he saw the absurd ambiguity of that remark. Although he could not help giving it the homage of a grin himself, he almost loved Forbes for remaining so grave. Lack of humour could be endearing. "Yes, Charlie," he hurried on, "we all have them. Thanks to our good sensible wives mostly, they die in the bud."

"My wife respects my ideals, Mr Fisher."

Mr Fisher didn't believe it. "You're lucky, Charlie," he murmured.

When he had seen his visitor off the headmaster tottered back to his desk. First he lit a cigarette and puffed at it with cancer-defying greed; then he snatched up the telephone and rang up his crony Bob Black, head of Oldlands Primary.

"Is that you, Bob?" he said. "Jack Fisher here."

Black had a big, loud, cheerful voice.

"Hello, Jack," he cried. "How's it going? Ticking off the days, eh?"

"Bob, thank God you sound as coarse and selfish and brutal as usual."

"What's going on?" asked Bob, laughing.

"I've just had a session with Charlie Forbes."

"Good old Charlie. What's biting him now? Last time he was objecting to your unchristian practice of allowing pupils to be strapped who'd forgotten their Bibles."

"You remember little Curdie? You sent him on to me a year ago."

"One of my brightest ever."

"Yes, but would you call him an example of magnanimity and indomitability?"

"Jack, I wouldn't even call myself that if I could get my tongue round them."

They laughed.

"I don't think I'd even call Charlie that," he added.

They laughed again.

"He's a nice enough fellow," said Bob, "but an awful humbug."

"Curdie's a sly wee rogue though, isn't he?"

"Isn't he just? Have you met his mother?"

"No. She's not one of the ambitious mammas who pester me about their sons' careers."

"No, she wouldn't be. But you've missed a treat, Jack. A genuine horror. Crafty as auld Nick's wife. Fat, too, like Charlie himself. Stinks. Her husband ran away from her years ago; no wonder."

"But she's got another, hasn't she?"

"Yes." The laughter went out of Bob's voice. "I wouldn't joke about him. He's a cripple, from birth I should think. I saw him once on the street; you know, Jack, my own legs felt fankled afterwards. But it doesn't stop him from getting drunk. A pair of beauties, I'm afraid. You can't help feeling sorry for young Curdie. He's got a younger brother here now, but he's a different type altogether: always greeting and utterly brainless. But why the sudden interest in Curdie? What's he done now?"

"Can't tell you, Bob. Sorry. It's a secret between me and Charlie. Let's say he's taking an interest in Curdie."

"Nothing wrong with that, if it's an intelligent interest."

"I'm afraid it isn't."

Bob paused. "I suppose, Jack, he's been at you to put in a word for him?"

"He has, Bob."

"Me, too. But the poor blighter always makes it sound as if it was me that was begging the favour."

"That's Charlie all right."

"Has he missed the boat now for good, d'you think?"

"Well, Bob, could he be entrusted with responsibility?"

"No, Jack, he couldn't. By the way, what's the latest about Walter Biddell?"

And they went on to discuss a fellow headmaster recently outmanoeuvred in a promotion campaign.

CHAPTER
TWO

The Forbes suburban sanctuary was one of a scheme of houses as alike and as architecturally interesting as match-boxes. Theirs was fortunate in that in front of it were open fields, across which hills could be seen in the distance. Not far away was a farm complete with midden, so that with a west wind came the smell of dung, pleasing Charlie in certain of his moods, and Mary in none. Within easy strolling distance was a wood with a lover's walk, where pheasants were sometimes seen; a stream flowed through it, a haunt of wagtails.

Their garden was tiny, which Charlie regretted in theory but welcomed in practice: he was too big in the belly, and too assiduous a planter of exotic hopes, to be zealous in the cultivation of leeks or even gladioli; but he liked to watch Mary plant, weed, mow, and chase neighbours' cats. Those neighbours themselves were much too close: five other gardens bordered on the Forbeses, so that on summer evenings it was no place for solitary contemplation.

No flower to Charlie was lovelier than his wife. Small, nicely plump, pink-cheeked, pleasantly smiling, black-haired with streaks of white, neat and assured in all her movements, whether walking along the avenue carrying a shopping basket or dancing a Duke of Perth, she was popular with her neighbours and saw to it that they respected her and her family. Whatever opinions they had about her husband, whatever smiles of good-natured derision he evoked, had to be hidden from her. She knew that those opinions and smiles existed, she even thought they were in some instances justified, and certainly she could not always keep free from annoyance at Charlie; but loyalty, good sense, self-respect, and affection, had so far enabled her to express that annoyance with tact and discretion. Nevertheless she often thought and sometimes said, with a little asperity, that she didn't have two children, she had three.

As soon as he came home from school that day he noticed that she was rather cross. When he inquired, fondly, she said she felt tired, that was all; she needed a holiday. At the tea table she scolded the children oftener than usual.

It should have been obvious to Charlie that he should have postponed the discussion about Tom Curdie; but even if it had occurred to him he would have rejected it on the grounds that where diplomacy was needed trust could not exist.

After tea, the dishes washed and dried, with Charlie enthusiastically helping, the children out at play again, he suggested a walk in the sunshine, for it had turned out a fine evening. She consented, on conditions: he wasn't to take her where she would have to cross ploughed fields or clamber over fences or — she laughed as she said this — help to pull him through when he got stuck. That picture of him fast by the belly and behind on barbs was unflattering, but it could be substantiated. The final condition was that he must wear his good flannels and new sports jacket. She herself would wear her new fawn summer coat. In it she looked charming, as he told her; but, as she told herself, she also looked cool, wary, and a shade pugnacious. From her point of view this stroll, like every other stroll in the district, was not merely for fresh air and exercise and the pleasure of birdsong; it was also for the informing of all neighbours in gardens or behind curtains that the Forbeses were as good as they.

They approached the farm. Mary grumbled as usual about the stench and the dilapidated outhouses that spoiled the appearance of the suburb. In one of those outhouses was kept a huge white bull which had won prizes: it was called Ardlamont Pride. The top part of the door was usually open, so that passers-by could see that massive melancholy head with the ringed nose and tearful eyes. Charlie was always fascinated. He could never pass, even when Mary was with him. Now this evening he went over, leant through the door, patted the great head, and spoke to it caressingly, as another person might have spoken to a kitten.

Mary at all times found the brute disgusting and terrifying. Sometimes she would linger and tease her husband as he admired it, but this evening she walked impatiently away, leaving him, and the Pride, gazing after her with similar expressions of regret.

16

Lingering had been one mistake; hurrying to make up was another. People she knew and didn't much like were watching. Although she agreed with him in principle that the tittle-tattle of such neighbours ought not to be heeded, still, being a sensitive woman, it galled her to catch a glimpse, through their eyes, of herself being neglected for a miry brute of a bull, and then being rejoined at an eager taurian gallop.

He arrived panting.

"There was no need to run, Charlie," she said. "If you like people laughing at you, I don't."

He turned and gazed after those poor clods without imagination who could not endure to see a man in a public place running after his wife in his joy to be by her side.

"You've got something to tell me," she said. "What is it?"

All along he had suspected that she had had one of her intuitive premonitions. It was not necessarily a bad sign.

Behind them the Pride bellowed.

"Well, there is something, Mary," he confessed, laughing.

"I knew it the minute you came in tonight."

She was referring of course to his concentration upon a propitiatory form of words; especially during the dish-drying had he sought it. That it was necessary did not of course belie his proud claim to Mr Fisher that she was very generous, and also that she respected his ideals. Like every other woman of spirit, Mary wished all his words to be a form of wooing.

"Well?" she asked.

"Mary, my dear, you've heard me talk about a boy called Tom Curdie?"

"You talk about so many of your pupils, Charlie, I can't be expected to remember them all."

"He's special, Mary. A very clever boy, from Donaldson's Court."

"Isn't he the one on probation for stealing?"

"That's him," he said eagerly.

"All right, what about him?"

"Perhaps I've spoken about his strange smile, his indomitable spirit?"

"Perhaps you have, Charlie."

He decided to plunge. "I made a vow today, Mary, one that I regard as solemn."

She waited.

"I vowed to take Tom Curdie with me to Towellan this summer."

"With you, Charlie? Are you going by yourself this year?"

"I meant, of course, with us. Provided you are agreeable."

"So I'm to have a say, Charlie?"

"You always have a say, Mary."

"And it's just as well for you, Charlie."

He remembered Mr Fisher's words about good, sensible wives.

"He's a thief," she said, with indignation.

"Because of corrupting influences, surely. It's those influences I hope to save him from. Consider where he lives, Mary. Mr Fisher himself said that if he had a pet tiger he wouldn't let it go into Donaldson's Court."

"Every child that lives in a slum isn't a thief. But why has it got to be you, Charlie? There are lots of them on your staff better able to afford it."

"Financially, yes."

"Didn't you tell me his mother lives with a man who's not her husband?"

"Yes, but that's not Tom's fault."

"I don't care whose fault it is, Charlie. I've got to protect my own children. He'll have seen and heard the most filthy things."

"Yes, Mary, he will have."

"He'll not be clean. He'll have lice. He'll swear. He'll lie. He'll have all kinds of disgusting habits."

"No, no," he cried. "He's not like that at all."

"What did Mr Fisher say?"

He did not answer; his face told her.

"I thought so, Charlie. And all the other teachers would say the same, not to mention the police." She softened her voice. "You dream too much about what should be, Charlie; you don't see what really is."

His whole being then seemed checked, suffocated, as if its necessary atmosphere was removed. He knew that atmosphere was his wife's support, approval, and loyalty.

She thought he looked like Alistair when denied some expensive toy.

"Apart from anything else, Charlie," she said, "look at the extra work it'd mean for me. I grumble enough as it is about the holiday just being a change of sinks for me."

"I do my share."

"You always mean to, I'll grant you that."

"I wash dishes." And then he realised that by introducing this pettiness he was yielding victory, not to her, but to that prevailing meanness of spirit which, however unwittingly, she represented then.

"A thousand women in my place, Charlie, would all give the same answer."

"I thought my wife was one in a thousand," he said humbly.

She was touched. "You're asking what's not fair, Charlie."

"I need your help, Mary," he said desperately.

She understood that he had made this thing far more important to him than he should.

"Charlie, my mother might be going with us."

"I thought she said she wasn't."

"She just said she might not be. As a matter of fact, I think she'll come."

"Well, even if she did there'd still be room for him in the hut."

"And a lot more work for me."

"I promise I'd do my share." He tried to laugh, to speak lightly. "If I fail in other things, Mary my dear, at least let me succeed in this."

She supposed he was referring to his failure to be promoted, and she wondered if this taking of the boy to Towellan wasn't a last desperate move to attract the favour of councillors.

"Have you asked him?" she asked. "The boy, I mean."

"I couldn't till I had your consent."

"Would he go?"

"I don't know."

"Perhaps he works during the holidays."

"It's possible."

"His people would object to losing his wages."

"I expect they would." He sighed. "It would seem that the circumstances of the world are all against my keeping my vow."

"Yes, Charlie, I think they are."

"So your verdict is: no?"

"I'm afraid so."

"Very well. Shall we say no more about it?"

"That suits me, Charlie."

He sighed again, and smiled, and put on his martyr's face.

No more was said about it until they were in their bedroom. He was peevishly struggling to loose a knot in his shoe-lace, caused by his inefficient bow-tying. She had her back to him.

"Are you really serious about wanting this boy Curdie to come with us?" she asked.

He turned round, astonished and disconcerted.

"So serious, Mary, that my reputation is involved."

She let the exaggeration pass. "Will it really do any good?" It was a double-edged question, and she looked at him to see if he understood. She thought he did.

"Yes, Mary, it will, a great deal of good, I'm sure of it."

"If we had him for a week, would that do?"

"I thought, a fortnight."

"Any trouble, and he goes home at once?"

"Certainly. But he won't give any trouble, Mary; I could swear to that."

"All right, we'll try it."

He jumped up, one shoe on, one off, and embraced her. "Thank you, Mary. I know you're doing this for my sake, and I'm very grateful."

"Don't let's talk about it any more tonight, Charlie. I'm tired."

When Charlie at last slept, after wrestling with qualms, he dreamed. In a green hilly field a boy sat on a huge white bull with his fist full of lice. The bull's face was like Charlie's own, but the boy's could never be seen clearly enough to be identified. In the background, bluer than ever he had seen it in reality, shone the Firth.

CHAPTER
THREE

An aesthete, as well as its humanitarian owner, would have been shocked had Mr Fisher's pet tiger wandered into Donaldson's Court. There its sleek skin, indigenous to jungle striped with sun and shadow, would have been shamed, and its fastidious paws polluted, by the garbage, filth, and overflow from broken privies. The splendour and beauty of the great beast would have been extinguished. In the same way, of course, it could be and often was objected that the more intricate, more fragile, and diviner beauty of the human body and mind was also shamed and polluted by such surroundings. But the humans had the advantage in that, being domiciled there for generations, they had undergone a debasement that softened the contrast. Newly-born babies in their prams, if washed, looked pathetically alien there; but in a short time, in two years or less, they had begun to acquire the characteristics which would enable them to survive amidst that dirt and savagery, but which naturally detracted a great deal from their original beauty. By manhood or womanhood they were as irretrievably adapted to their environment as the tiger to his. Hence aesthetes, humanitarians, moralists, and politicians, whilst still appreciating the tragedy, had it presented to them in a tolerable manner. Slumdom was hideous; but then the people who lived there were slum-dwellers.

On a wet afternoon two days after Mr Forbes had made his vow, through the pend that led into Donaldson's Court, walked one of its inhabitants, distinguishable from most by his bright, wary, uncommitted eyes. He was Tom Curdie. In one pocket he had a letter from Forbes addressed to his mother although she could hardly read, and in another an apple lifted from a box outside a fruiterer's; this was for his brother Alec who had been off school that day through illness.

There was another inhabitant in the pend. An old black cat crouched in a hole against the wall, sheltering from rain and cruelties. It seemed afraid to close its eyes, and kept shivering as if in a nightmare of gigantic rats. It had been kicked out by someone. Soon it would be found dead and its carcase swung by the tail by boys to make girls scream, before being tossed into some dustbin where the scavengers would discover it with oaths of outrage.

Tom went over, squatted, and, heedless of the scabs visible under its fur, stroked it. Suspicious of kindness, it mewed in misery at being too weak to slink away. He did not speak either to reassure or sympathise. Pity was never shown by him, only comradeship. For any creature whom he accepted as his comrade he would lie, steal, or suffer. This old cat was such a comrade. Recognising its hunger, and having only the apple reserved for Alec, he did not know what to do. Then, biting off a piece, he placed it under the cat's mouth. It

24

mewed and sniffed, but did not eat. He knew that his presence, his human smell threatening treachery and cruelty, put it off. He rose up, therefore, and padded out into the rain. There he looked back. The cat, not much liking apple, was nevertheless eating. He smiled in approval. Never to whine; to accept what came; to wait for better; to take what you could; to let no one, not even yourself, know how near to giving in you were: these were his principles by which he lived, and he honoured them in this old dying cat.

To reach his house, two storeys up, he had to climb a common stair wet with overflow from a privy. A stench of damp, decay, and urine, lay sour and thick on the air. He was passed by an old man, snivelling and squeaking, whose face looked like an apple out of which several bites had been taken. He was nearly blind. It was his custom to swing a blow at any person passing him, and when he missed, as he usually did, he broke into a horrible weeping and struck at himself. He drank methylated spirits and melted boot polish, and was crazy.

Tom easily dodged aside, without laughing, as some did, or swearing, like others. He gazed after the sobbing old man without fear, anger, or disgust. There were many such persons in the Court and the surrounding tenements. He knew them and their vices and despairs. He passed no judgment, but they were not his comrades. They had all long ago given in, and wanted him to give in, too.

It was Alec who opened the door. As soon as he saw Tom he began to whimper. He had a large sore at the side of his mouth, and looked ill.

Apparently not heeding the self-piteous whines of his brother, Tom entered the single-roomed house. No one else was there. His mother, with his half-sister of three, was out visiting; she would be drinking beer and playing cards.

Alec had been alone in the house for three hours; now he followed his brother about, as plaintive and possessive as a kitten.

"Did you bring me onything?" he asked. "You said you would."

Tom handed him the apple.

"I don't like aipples very much," whined Alec.

"It's good for you."

"There's a bite oot o'it."

"I wanted to see if it was sweet."

"Is it sweet?"

"Aye."

Alec took a bite. "It's no' very sweet," he grumbled. "Did you steal it, Tom?"

"I took it."

"Shoogle says taking's juist the same as stealing."

Shoogle was their foster-father. Imposed on him as an infant, the nickname had come to be used even by his mother, and now his three-year-old daughter lisped it. He worked in a rope factory.

"Shoogle's feart for you, Tom."

Alec hee-hee'd at that astonishing fear inspired by his brother who was smaller even than Shoogle and not so strong.

"Will I read a comic to you?" asked Tom.

Alec agreed eagerly; he could not read himself well enough to enjoy it.

They sat side-by-side on a chair whose stuffing and springs were visible. Soon Alec was laughing as his brother read about the antics of the characters in the comic. But Tom's own mind was only partly on what he was reading. He was also wondering what Forbes's true reason was for so strange an invitation. The teacher had spoken about good food, fresh air, and scenery; he had said they would do Tom good, physically and morally. Tom had understood very well what he had meant, but he could not see what Forbes hoped to get out of it. He knew that Forbes was supposed to be conceited and rather stupid, and that other teachers laughed at him behind his back. Was this invitation then just an act of conceit and stupidity? Or was Forbes really trying to be kind?

Once before Tom had been befriended by a teacher. It was in the Primary. Miss McIntosh, who was always bothering him with kindness, one day brought clothes for him; they had belonged to her young brother. Tom had accepted them, but he had taken them straight after school to a junkshop where the man had given him ninepence for them. Next morning, when Miss McIntosh had whispered why he was not wearing them, he had announced, loudly so that all the class would hear, what he had done with them. He had expected her to strike him with her hand or the strap; indeed, he had wanted her to. Instead she had just stood and stared at him, with tears in her eyes. She had not reported him to Mr Black the headmaster. He had been nine then. Even now he could not forgive her for her pity. She had come nearest to coaxing him to give in.

Forbes was different: he could be laughed at. Besides, it was more likely that Forbes was offering to take him just to show off, to prove that he was better than the other teachers who would never think of taking with them a boy from Donaldson's Court. From many things Forbes had said in class, and from overhearing remarks passed by other teachers, Tom knew that the fat English master was conceited about his championing of people oppressed, such as slaves, boy chimney sweeps, women in mines, foxes hunted by hounds, boys severely strapped, and children living in slums. He would hold up a lesson to display his indignation at those oppressions. It was always an opportunity for some boys to read comics under their desks, or do next day's Latin exercise, or just doze. One of the commonest charges against Forbes by his pupils was that he wasted such a lot of time.

Tom knew very well that the majority of children were far more fortunate than he, but he had never envied them. Envy, like pity, was not in his creed. What he hoped to do or to become was apart altogether from what others did or became. To have been envious would have been to become involved and so weakened. His success, if ever it came, must owe nothing to anyone.

So far he had preserved this lonely independence. Not even Alec, or Peerie Whitehouse and Chick Mackie, the two members of his gang, had been allowed to violate it. Shame made no breach in him: he had none, neither for himself nor for others. For instance, he knew that the mothers of the other boys in his class wore hats and silk stockings and did not get drunk. His own mother, on the contrary, wore her hair lank and lousy about her ears and sometimes over her eyes. Usually her legs were bare, mottled with dirt and varicose veins. She was fat like Forbes, with her belly swollen and her breasts shrunken, so that when she stripped to the waist to wash at the sink she did not look like a woman at all. When she spoke she slavered, so that every three or four words she had to suck in and swallow. Several of her teeth were missing, making those oral noises of fatuous sorrow and mirth all the louder. She often made foolish jokes and wept silly tears, especially when drunk; then she would lament the early days of her marriage before her two sons were born, and before fat, like a curse from heaven, had fallen upon her, driving away her man who had disliked fat, even on ham.

Such was his mother, but Tom was not ashamed of her; neither was he fond or proud. She was a phenomenon he had known since birth. All he owed her was life, a gift shared by lice and rats. If she gave him an order which he thought foolish, inconvenient, or unnecessary, he would ignore it; as he would any appeal which it did not suit him to answer. She might wheedle, threaten, or cry she was going to commit suicide, it made no difference. Since the age of five he had pleased himself.

As for her bedmate, Shoogle Kemp, he was of no account.

That left Molly his half-sister, who was the only creature Tom feared; not because of her vicious little nails which could cause suppurating scratches, or her shrieking rages, but because she had once been a chuckling baby whom he had liked to push about in a battered pram.

He was diverted from these thoughts by Alec tugging peevishly at his arm.

"You're no' reading, Tom. Whit's up?"

"I was thinking."

"Whit aboot, Tom?"

It was then that the idea came into Tom's mind. Merely to go with Forbes to Towellan would be purposeless. Why not then take Alec with him, and Peerie and Chick? They could sleep in the gang's tent. No shopkeeper there would know them. There would be farms with henhouses, fields with potatoes, the sea with fish. It would pay Forbes back.

But some money would be needed.

Tea that evening was a typical meal. Mrs Curdie was almost drunk, and since her lover objected to her anticipating him in that condition she had to cringe with penitence. Molly, who had toothache, screamed at everybody and emptied her mug of tea over Alec, who pretended to have been scalded and howled. Shoogle, with sleeves rolled up, revealing puny tattoo'd forearms, ignored all the hubbub to concentrate on giving as many passionately bitter reasons as he could for rejecting the melted potted head which Queenie, with tipsy economy, had bought cheap.

A lull came. Molly had fallen asleep on the floor. It appeared she had already been dosed with whisky to allay the ache.

"One of the teachers," said Tom, "wants to take me with him on his holidays."

His mother was furtively eating the potted head that Shoogle had refused. She looked up, with astonishment in her bloodshot eyes giving way to surmise, horror, and calculation.

"God, did you hear that, Shoogle?" she asked.

"I'm no' deaf."

"But whit's the idea?" She made faces intended to indicate abominations for which there were names. "D'you think that's it?"

"I've read that it's worse among educated men," he said. "Actors and lawyers and teachers and even ministers, they're all at it."

"Especially ministers," she agreed. "You read aboot them every Sunday in the *News of the World*."

Then she turned to Tom who had watched her every ogle, smirk, leer, and gesture.

"Wha is he?" she asked.

"Mr Forbes."

"Aye, but whit's he like? Does he use scent on his hankies?"

"That would prove nothing," said Shoogle. "I used to put scent on mine."

She forgot the wickedness of the world then to gawk at him in love and wonder. "Did ye, Shoogle?"

He disregarded her to address Tom.

"This man, Forbes, does he ever ask boys to wait after four?"

Tom nodded. He knew what was being hinted at.

"I mean," whispered Shoogle, after a pause in which his shrivelled face, for all its work-dirt and unshavenness, looked as vindictively wise as a High Court Judge's, "does he ask single boys?"

"Yes."

"Would you credit it?" cried Mrs Curdie. "Right under the heidie's nose! We send oor weans to school to be educated and that's whit we get. In my day teachers had whiskers and bowler hats. It was wee lassies they were after then; that was bad enough, but it was mair natural." She put her hand at her mouth and whispered behind it. "Whit d'you think, Shoogle? Would this fellow pay onything to keep oor mooths shut?"

"That would be blackmail, Queenie. D'you want two years in jail?"

"Naebody would ken."

Suddenly he banged his fist on the table.

"For Christ's sake," she beseeched, "don't wake up Molly."

"I don't care if I woke up the deid. Listen to me, Queenie."

"I'm listening, Shoogle."

"We've got a problem to consider. This place we live in, whit is it? I'll tell you. It's a dump, a bluidy rotten dump."

"There's worse, Shoogle. We havenae got rats chewing at oor lugs during the night."

"Are we human beings or beasts?"

32

She sighed. "They say it takes five quid a week to feed a greyhound."

"I've lived here a' my days," went on Shoogle. "I'm a product. Look at me, for God's sake, a product." He looked down at his legs. "When I was a wee boy, younger than Alec there, a man had me up on a platform at a political meeting. That's whit he christened me then: a product."

"He had nae right to dae sich a thing."

"He's deid noo," said Shoogle, "but before he dee'd he had a job worth three thousand pounds a year."

"Feather your ain nest, it's the same everywhere, Shoogle."

"So we've got to be careful, Queenie. This man Forbes might be a genuine Christian."

"I thought they were extinct, like giraffes."

"Giraffes are no' extinct."

"Weel, they should be, wi' necks like lamp-posts."

She sniggered at her own jokes, but he did not respond. Seriousness was, in her opinion, his greatest handicap; it crippled him worse than his twisted legs.

"If Forbes is doing this for Tom because he's a Christian," said Shoogle, "then there's nae problem. But if it's for the ither reason, there is a problem."

She was shocked. "You're no suggesting you'd let him go, if . . .?"

"I'm saying there's a problem. Whit we've got to do is to balance the harm that might come to the boy if he goes wi' Forbes, against the harm that'll come to him if like you and me he never gets away frae this kind of life. He's got brains. Every teacher he's had has said so.

Given a chance he micht get oot and do weel. But who's to gie him that chance, Queenie? No' you or me, for we're no' able. There's nae candidate but this fellow Forbes."

She turned towards her son who had been listening inscrutably.

"This one'll please himself," she whined.

"I've to get your permission," said Tom.

"You're my ain son. I can mind the very hour you were born. But I ken less aboot you now than I did then. You've got nae fondness for me, I ken that. You've got nae respect and nae pity. When did I ever see a ha'penny o' the money you get at the dairy? Why should me and Shoogle worry aboot you? You'll gang to hell in your ain way. Let Forbes tak' you. He'll be sorry. You're one that'll never pay if the price doesnae suit you."

He chose that moment to say: "Mrs Forbes is going, and they've got two children."

His mother's reaction was not anger at being deceived, or relief at having her fears dispelled, but rather solicitude at Shoogle's peculiar disappointment. She was trying to console him when Molly woke up and began to scream for attention.

CHAPTER
FOUR

In school June was a good month for money. Class photographs had to be paid for, at half a crown each. Mr Forbes, for example, as form-master of A Boys, had to collect over a period of days more than four pounds. But Mr Todd, as treasurer for the Sports, received in small change more than any other teacher. Accordingly, one day towards the end of June he found himself encumbered with a canvas bag containing about five pounds in pennies, threepences, and sixpences. It was bulky and heavy. To take it home was unthinkable: not only would the pocket of his new suit be permanently misshaped, but his principle of never confusing duty with leisure would be betrayed. During the last period that day, while IA boys were busy at sums, he grumbled to Mr Duncan.

They tried to remember to speak in whispers.

"Give it to Bud," suggested Duncan.

"Have you ever tried," muttered Todd, "giving Bud money to keep for you after banking hours? The bugger says it's against his union's regulations."

Bud was the school janitor.

"Give it to the boss then."

"Why the hell should I? I'm as capable of looking after it as he is; more capable, I should hope."

"All right then, keep it in your desk. It'll be safe enough for one night."

"Look who's in the second row over there."

Duncan looked and saw Tom Curdie, apparently engrossed in his work which involved sums much larger than five pounds.

"Charlie's darling," he whispered.

It was now known that Forbes was taking Curdie to Towellan.

"Whom I trust that far," said Todd, and he portioned off on his finger an area that would have cramped a flea. "I wouldn't be surprised if the little bastard was sitting there listening to every word." Suddenly he let out a roar. "Curdie, bring your jotter here."

Tom seemed startled at being disturbed in his trance of arithmetic. "Me, sir?"

"There's only one Curdie, isn't there?"

He came out, carrying his jotter, which was dirty and crumpled. Having no bag or case, all his books had to be carried under his jacket.

"Filth!" roared Todd. "Am I supposed to handle that? Drop it on the desk and then keep your distance."

Tom dropped his jotter on the desk and stood aside. Many in the class laughed. He neither blushed nor sulked.

"Brazen as a brass monkey," growled Todd.

Duncan nodded; he felt sorry for the boy, but didn't think it worth while to say so.

To get out his book containing the answers Todd had to open the drawer in which the money-bag lay. He tried to smother it under other papers.

The first ten sums were correct.

"All right," said Todd. "Take it and get back to your seat." Waiting till the boy had returned, he whispered: "Better to make sure. You never know what's in that one's head."

"No," agreed Duncan.

"A pity," admitted Todd grudgingly. "One of the best heads in the school."

Had they been able to study Tom's plans they would have found no reason to lower their estimate of his intelligence. Before leaving the classroom he had arranged how he would re-enter it late that night. The locked door would cause him no trouble. If he knocked a little hole in the glass he could put in his hand and unfasten the bolt that kept the whole door and part of the wall from sliding open. He would come alone. His two confederates, Peerie and Chick, being backward at lessons, attended another school. Therefore they wouldn't know their way about in the dark, and unfamiliarity meant clumsiness, which meant noise. Besides, the joy of having a school at his mercy might set Chick off upon some pranks of revenge, such as scribbling dirty words or drawings on blackboards. He and Peerie might afterwards boast, and boasting more than anything else broke vows of silence.

All that evening Tom acted so normally and calmly that nobody could have suspected he was about to embark upon the most daring and ambitious theft of his career. His mother and Shoogle having gone out, he had to wash Molly and put her to bed. Her toothache made her more cantankerous than ever, so that he had to stand beside her cot, holding her hand and humming a song about a baby stolen by fairies in the Highlands. After she was asleep he sat by the fire reading a comic in a low voice to Alec, until the latter was too drowsy to listen and had to be put to bed. Then he was able to write out the two hundred lines that Miss Strang had given him: "Hygiene is not a luxury". At one point, during the writing of the one hundred and eightieth line, his smile faded, and he sat for minutes staring at the tap as it dripped into the rusty sink. As he resumed writing his smile returned.

Before his parents returned, about eleven o'clock, he himself was in bed, where Alec was already sound asleep. They were drunk and amorous, she giggling to him to wait till they were in bed, he huffish and embittered at such patience. After the scuffles on the rag-rug under the hissing gas, they at last crawled into their bed, where there were more scuffles, giggles, groans, and heavings. All this time Tom lay in an aseptic indifference: dogs, cats, rats, sparrows, flies, human beings; he had seen them all at their copulations, and whether these were shameful or ugly or sordid or just comical, as other boys argued, he was not concerned enough to say.

At last the room was quiet save for his mother's snores and Molly's snuffles. Rising, he put on his jacket and sandshoes, and left the house. The stairs were dark for all the stairhead gasmantles were broken, but he slipped down confident as a ghost. At one place he had to step over a body sobbing and moaning in desolation and abandonment. But that was not where he was to haunt, so he glided past without even wondering who the outcast was.

To reach the school one lighted main street had to be crossed, where policemen patrolled. He crossed amidst the shadows, and soon was slinking down the side street, from which it was safest to enter the school. Climbing over the railings into the playground was easy, but somehow crossing the playground turned out to be difficult in a way he had never anticipated. There was no physical obstacle; on the contrary, it was the complete emptiness and stillness that disturbed him. That afternoon the playground had been thronged with hundreds of shouting, happy boys. Now in spite of himself he saw them again, and was moved. It certainly wasn't because he was going to take the money they had paid for their photographs and sports fees; and it wasn't because they were his schoolmates, sharing the same classrooms and using the same books. He could not say why it was, but as he gazed at the still playground and remembered the boisterous crowd which had filled it, that inexplicable emotion touched him for a minute, so much so, that when he reached the grating which had to be scaled to gain the upper verandah where Todd's room was, he was astonished and dismayed to find his arms and legs without strength or willingness to climb. He waited by the grating, holding on to its bars like a prisoner, as he subdued that treacherous weakness. Not to give in had been his pride, his faith, his sustenance, and so far it had not failed him. Now for no reason, just because the playground was empty as it was bound to be at half-past one in the morning, he was in danger of surrendering. It must be Forbes's fault. Ever since accepting the invitation to Towellan he had not felt safe; Forbes had been pestering him with kindness.

The hole in the glass had to be as small and neat as possible. Glass falling was noisy, and the janitor's black dog in its kennel had keen ears. Todd's room was first. With a screwdriver he gently broke the glass with the handle. He had a cloth ready to catch any fragments that fell outside. With the cloth wrapped round his wrist he thrust in his hand and withdrew the bolt. Going along to the handle of the door he tugged it, and so simply, as if the whole mechanism was in league with him it slid open. In a moment he was inside, the door shut again.

There was plenty of light from the lamps in the street. Yonder, in the second row, was his own desk. Here, by the blackboard, was the teacher's, containing, he hoped, that bag of money. On the board was chalked the sum worked out by Todd days ago. As he glanced at desk after desk he recalled who sat at each; none of them was his friend or comrade.

He did not hurry. Panic meant mistakes. That weakness shown in the playground must be overcome.

At last he approached Todd's desk. Prising open the drawer took longer than was necessary, not just because he didn't want to make a noise, but also because he

40

wanted to do as little damage as possible. Not even anxiety lest Todd after all had taken the money home caused him to become reckless.

The lock was broken, the drawer ready to be opened. Calmly he opened it and felt inside. Sure enough, there under some papers was the bag of coins, reminding him of the great lump that old Jack Tomkin who lived in the Court had under his chin. But Jack's lump was without value, except in the imaginations of fascinated children where it was spent again and again. It could not buy steamer tickets or food or camp equipment. This other lump, growing out of Mr Todd's astonished mouth, could buy all those things. As Tom picked it up he held it against his throat, and during that moment seemed to become old Jack with his kitten's voice, his painful laughter, and his lifetime of disease and hardship in the Court. With a shudder he took the bag away from his throat and crammed it into his pocket. To stop it jingling he stuffed in with it some pages from an old jotter.

Though he hadn't allowed Peerie and Chick to come with him because they might play tell-tale tricks, he could not resist playing one himself. There was a bottle of red ink in the desk. Taking it out, and removing the cap, he went over to the door and let ink drip on to the floor and broken glass under the hole. From there to the desk he laid a trail of ink spots, smiling as he imagined Todd's satisfaction that one of the burglars at any rate had had to pay in blood.

It was while he was wiping his finger-prints off the ink bottle that he realised how unwise he had been. He had offered two suggestions to his enemies. They would look for blood on his hands and on the soles of his shoes. So far he had avoided that, but what if, in entering one of the other rooms, he scratched his hand, however slightly? It would be as good as a confession. Todd would examine the wrists of every boy in the school. It would be safer not to try to enter any other room.

Yet there was one room he must enter: Forbes's room. To pass it would be to show himself in some way afraid of the fat English teacher. It would be like admitting he was grateful, and he knew that if ever he were to be grateful to anybody, his confidence in himself would be destroyed.

In Forbes's drawer, in a little box, were six half-crowns. As Tom picked them up he remembered how the photographer, a small, thick-lipped Jew in a bowler hat, had arranged the boys according to size, making good-humoured jokes about each in turn. When he had come to Tom he had noticed, with one soft brown-eyed glance, how more poorly dressed than the others he was, and had, without a joke, pushed him into a position where only his face would be visible. Perhaps it had been done out of a desire to make the photograph more saleable. But with the half-crowns in his hand Tom wondered whether it would be the small Jew who would lose them.

He tried two other rooms but got nothing. The teachers, one of them Mr Duncan, must have taken their money home with them. It was a precaution he would have taken himself; yet somehow, in the silent classrooms at two in the morning, it disturbed him. It represented what might keep him in Donaldson's Court all his life. The sensible calculation of the world was in this obvious removing of the money to a safe place, this trusting of nobody even for a night. Everybody did it, except simpletons like Forbes. People put their money in banks for safety. Shillings were never found, like dandelions, in cracks in the pavement. Why then should he be concerned by this customary act on the part of Mr Duncan and Mr Timpson? He knew it was foolishness, caused perhaps by want of sleep, yet he could not help picturing the two teachers standing by their desks, laughing as he looked in vain. "Nothing for you, Curdie, nothing at all, nothing." He might grin at his own stupidity in letting his imagination tease him thus, he might slap the bag in his pocket, it was no good, he couldn't throw off the burden of all those millions of people who kept their money safe, with none for him.

He was so tired and so oppressed by the loneliness of the streets, that as he opened the door and smelled the familiar fug, and heard his mother snore, he was almost betrayed into a sigh of relief, at being back again. Home was a word he would not use: all that it seemed to signify, comfort, security, help, and permanence, were absent there.

As he was undressing Molly stirred and whimpered for a drink. He went over and held her up to give her one.

His mother spoke from the bed. "Whit's that? Wha is it?"

"It's me," he said. "Molly wanted a drink."

"Did you gie her one?"

"Aye."

"That's a good boy. You're a good boy at hert. I didnae mean whit I said to you the night. You've got to look after yourself. Christ pity us." Repeating that prayer, with a long yawn, she sank back into sleep.

Within five minutes he was asleep, too.

CHAPTER
FIVE

Forbes was always one of the earliest teachers to arrive in the morning. It was not only hypocritical, he said, it was downright dishonest, to inculcate punctuality in children, indeed to punish them for not observing it, and then not observe it oneself. His colleagues agreed, even those who frequently enough sneaked in by the back entrance after prayers had started; but in their prayers no blessings were asked for him.

The morning after the burglary, half an hour to the good, he walked up the steps at the front door, passed under the mitred head of the patron saint of the city, and entered the hall, where he was at once pounced on by Bud the janitor and informed that his room and the other three rooms in that wing of the building had been broken into and the locks of the desk-drawers forced. Bud then wanted to know if Forbes had left anything valuable in his desk, hinting strongly that, if he had, he was a mug.

"You teachers are too damned soft with them nooadays," said Bud.

"You wouldn't want to put the clock back," said Forbes.

It was a brave utterance, for he was wondering what had happened to the half-crowns which he had left in his drawer, an offering on the altar of trust.

"It'd be some boyish prank," he said, laughing. "How many straps are missing?"

"None. One of them cut his hand. There's blood all over Mr Todd's room. By God, he's one that'll make a proper song about it."

Todd's song, in one respect, was quite improper; it contained several oaths. Legs apart, he stood in the middle of the staffroom, pouring bucketfuls of ashes over his big bald commissar's head. As a green student, he roared, he had had a lead pencil, worth one penny, lifted from under his eyes. From that day he had made a vow that, all children being by nature tarry-fingered, nothing of his must ever be allowed near enough them to stick. Now at an age of ripest discretion and maturest cynicism, he had blundered, he had depended on trust. He deserved his arse kicked, but if it was left to him he would see to it that the arses of the culprits would be flayed and pulverised.

At first the headmaster would not leave it to him: the police were brought in. Two detectives came, looked, discovered the blood was red ink, found fault with the system of bolting the sliding door, and left with the insinuation that if any boys in the school were suspected it might be more profitable to leave their cross-examination in the hands of the teachers, in the first place at any rate. Altogether the police gave the impression that in the hundred or so burglaries perpetrated in the city that week, with the culprits still unearthed, this one was negligible, well down the list. As for Todd's four pounds eighteen shillings and fivepence ha'penny, they did not directly say they regarded its loss as a penance for his naïve trustfulness, but they implied it clearly enough to choke him with exasperation. They said nothing at all about Forbes's half-crowns, for the good reason that they did not know about these, he having decided to keep quiet about them to prevent ridicule, not of himself, but of the faith embodied in him. That Todd's trust had been violated was not surprising; the high proportion of cynicism in it made violation almost pardonable. But that his own had been was unaccountable and tragic. Todd had many ill-wishers in the district; but Forbes's former pupils, as well as his present ones, respected him, he knew, and appreciated his fairness towards them.

In the staff room it was suggested it might have been done by strangers.

"No," said Todd. "The buggers knew their way around too well for that. Besides, didn't they know the money was in the desk?" He turned round to look for Forbes, despondent in a corner. "Charlie," he cried, "I congratulate you."

"On what?" asked Forbes coldly.

"On having the intelligent meanness to keep your drawer like Mother Hubbard's cupboard. On not being like me, a simple trusting gomeril."

Forbes said nothing.

Todd addressed the company. "If he allows me a free hand, I'll have the truth, and the money, by four o'clock."

"Do you mean," asked Forbes hoarsely, "the map-room?"

"Yes, by God, Charlie, I do mean the map-room. In the old days we treated rogues as rogues. One at a time in the map-room, with a big Lochgelly. It never failed."

"Gestapo methods," said Forbes. "In your eyes is civilisation worth only four pounds eighteen and fivepence ha'penny?"

"Less than that, Charlie, when it's my money."

"At least you're frank."

"And that's better than being smug and phoney."

Some of the others were uneasy. One hurried in to divert Todd.

"Whom do you suspect, Bill?"

"You mean, number one?"

"Yes."

"Curdie, of IA."

"Why?"

"Because he's as sleekit as your granny's cat; and because he was almost cracking his dirty little ears to listen to what Jimmy Duncan and me were saying yesterday afternoon. That right, Jimmy?"

Duncan smiled. "He was doing his sums too, Bill."

"Of course. You'll never catch Curdie if you take him at his face value."

Forbes stood up. "I'm warning you now that if this boy is bullied over this I shall take it to the highest authorities."

"Who have, as we all know, Charlie, such a high opinion of your talents."

48

At that insult Forbes, with a dignity enhanced by his flowing black gown, left the room.

"Bloody fool," muttered Todd. "No wonder the public have no respect for us. No wonder we're looked on as a shower of auld wives."

"I can understand Charlie's feeling about Curdie," said Duncan.

"Jimmy, if I can pin this theft on the little bastard, Charlie ought to give me a public apology, and thank me into the bargain."

"Yes, but you've still to pin it on him."

"That red ink trick proved it. There's not another boy in this school with that kind of humour."

Two or three smiled as they recollected how, as blood, it had appeased his pride, and how, as red ink, it had outraged it.

"Bud and I have drawn up a list of the most likely," said Todd.

"Is it the total school roll you've got, Bill? Nothing else surely would satisfy Bud."

"Eleven names so far; but I'm open to suggestions."

"Alboe for a cert."

"And Johnstone of IIE."

"And big Alison."

"And Docherty of IIIB."

Other names were suggested.

"Got them all," cried Todd proudly, "every damned one. I've got a nose for rogues. Charlie would say it's because I'm one myself. Curdie's third on the list."

"I thought you said he was number one?"

"He is. But after a couple have been put through it he'll be in a sweat. Psychology."

"I can't say I've ever seen Curdie in a sweat," said Duncan.

Others agreed.

"Well, you'll see him in one today," said Todd.

When he went out there was a short silence.

"I can't help feeling sorry for wee Curdie," said someone.

"Yes," said another, "I find him harmless. I admit he's deep, but what's in him he keeps to himself, as far as I'm concerned."

"What's Charlie going to do?" asked a third. "If ever there was a crusader without a sword it's poor Charlie; and without a shield."

Forbes's request to be present at the interrogation of Tom Curdie was granted by Mr Fisher.

"Yes, Charlie," he said, "in the circumstances I think you've a right to hear what Curdie's got to say."

Todd, seated by the headmaster's side like the sinister adviser to some doted Renaissance prince, didn't agree. "I hope he's going to keep out of the questioning," he said.

"Of course. He just wants to hear what Curdie's got to say. In the circumstances I think it's reasonable."

As Todd grunted a quiet knock was heard at the door.

"Come in," called the headmaster.

Tom Curdie entered. No boy could have been more respectful, and properly aware that he stood in the presence of authority. Yet both Todd and Forbes caught the smile that for an instant flickered across the small earnest face. To Todd it indicated a depth of insolence, to Forbes indomitability. He had shown a little surprise on seeing Forbes there in the corner.

He addressed the headmaster.

"Did you want to see me, sir?"

"Yes, Tom. Mr Todd and I have a few questions to ask you. Just tell the truth."

"Yes, sir."

Todd had been smoking. Elaborately he took the cigarette out of his mouth, stubbed it on the ash-tray, and then began to feel through his pockets for his cigarette case. In his search for it he had to take out his black coiled belt, which he laid on the desk under Curdie's nose. That nose, however, showed no twitch of terror; indeed, the smile came and went again, as swiftly as before.

"You know what this is all about?" asked Todd, pleasantly.

"Not really, sir."

"You don't, eh? You haven't heard the school was broken into last night?"

"Yes, sir, I heard that. I saw the broken glass, and the detectives."

"You'd recognise them as detectives all right. Now, Curdie, I want you to account for every minute you spent yesterday between four o'clock and the time you went to bed. Now what did you do after you left school?"

"I went for a walk."

"Who with?"

"Just myself, sir."

"Where?"

"Along the banks of the Clyde."

"You'd arranged to meet somebody there. Who was it?"

"Nobody, sir. I just saw five swans."

Todd grinned, appreciating the stroke.

"After that, Tom, what did you do?" asked Mr Fisher, anxious to do his share of the questioning.

"I went — to where I live."

"Do you mean, you went home?"

Again the boy hesitated; then he nodded.

"Then why not say so?"

"All right," chipped in Todd. "You went home. Did you meet anybody on the way?"

"Nobody I spoke to, sir."

"Who was in the house when you got there?"

"Just my brother."

"What age is he?"

"Nine, sir. He's at Oldlands school."

"When did the others come in?"

"My mother and sister came in a wee bit after five."

"What about your father?"

"He's not my father."

"No. But you call him father, don't you?"

"No, sir."

"Then what do you call him?"

"Perhaps guardian?" suggested the headmaster.

Tom smiled: the term was never used, but it was so silly it would do.

"Did you all stay in all evening?" asked Todd.

"No, sir. My mother and guardian" — again he smiled — "went out about seven."

"And when did they come back?"

"Just before eleven, I think, sir. I was in bed."

"So you stayed in all evening, with your brother and sister? Why? It was a fine sunny evening."

"No, sir. It was wet."

"Yes, so it was. And yet you go a walk and talk to swans? What did you do all evening?"

"I read comics to my brother. Then I put my sister to bed — she's just three."

"I see." The headmaster spoke sadly.

"When they were in bed, what did you do?" asked Todd sharply.

"I wrote two hundred lines for Miss Strang. Then I read a book."

"What book?"

"It's called *Martin Rattler*. Mr Forbes lent it to me."

"I did lend him that book," said Forbes.

"What time did you go to bed?"

"About ten, sir."

Todd paused. "I'll tell you what you did, Curdie. You left your brother and sister sleeping, slipped out, met your pals, and came here. About half-past ten or so."

"No, sir."

"Let's see your hands."

Todd examined them carefully. They were not clean, they were calloused and scarred, but they had no red ink on them.

"Now," said Todd, about to produce his master-stroke, "the soles of your shoes."

Like an obedient dog tolerant of its master's foolishness, Curdie turned his back and held up his right foot so that the sole of his sandshoe could be seen. In it there was a hole, with the skin visible; but there was no trace of red ink. Nor was there any on his left.

"You're smart, Curdie," said Todd.

The boy seemed to bow his head a little in acknowledgement.

"But, by God, you're not taking me in," cried Todd. "I know you're guilty, and I'm warning you, your life in this school won't be worth living till you own up."

Suddenly Todd banged on the desk. It shocked his superior more than his victim. As Mr Fisher jumped, Curdie picked up some papers that had been sent flying.

"You're a born thief and liar, Curdie," roared Todd. "You're a credit to the slums that bred you. Now get out of my sight."

Curdie stood his ground, waiting till the headmaster dismissed him. His exit was as composed as his entrance.

Instantly Forbes was across the room.

"Mr Fisher," he cried, "you heard the threat that was offered to that boy."

"It's all most unfortunate," murmured the headmaster.

Todd sneered and lit a cigarette.

Forbes faced him. "I warn you," he said, "lay a finger on that child, and I shall personally charge you with assault. Good God, he's here to be educated, not terrified, humiliated, and bullied. We are supposed to be his allies, not his enemies."

54

"Charlie," said Todd, "I've been too long at the game to be taken in by such guff."

"Mr Todd, why do you have such a grudge against the child? He lacks every advantage in life, including a decent home. You saw how he avoids the very word."

"A neat trick, typical of Curdie."

"If you mean he did it to win pity, how wrong you are. No child in this school, in this whole city, seeks pity less."

The headmaster held up his hand. "Gentlemen, please remember where you are. It does seem to me that the boy's a disturbing influence. Perhaps the best solution would be to have him transferred to Brian Street."

"That's where he should have been sent to in the first place," said Todd.

Forbes was aghast. Such a transference would be educational chicanery. Brian Street was where pupils of low mental calibre were sent. Yet it would be easy enough to transfer Curdie, whose parents would certainly not object.

"It would be scandalous to send him there," he said. "The boy's got a first-rate intelligence."

"I'll tell you this, Charlie," said Todd. "He's guilty."

"You have no right to say that. You produced absolutely no proof."

"I could feel it. It's a knack I have, Charlie: a tingle runs up and down my spine. And while I'm at it, let me tell you something else. You don't take anybody in with your blethers about principle. You're as much on the make as any of us. The difference between you and me,

Charlie, is this: if I passed a blind beggar with a tinny I'd drop in a couple of coppers and pass on, without giving him another thought; but you'd be so damned indignant at such public misery and so busy blaming everybody else for it that you'd pass by without putting anything in at all."

Forbes was astonished. On the surface it was an accurate enough description.

"I'll tell you how I know, Charlie. I was just behind you once going up Buchanan Street. There was an old fellow with no eyes in his head and a row of medals on his chest. You gave him bags of sympathy, I could see that; but I had the feeling you were pretty displeased with him for sporting medals that he probably never won. It was a complicated business for you getting past him. For me it was easy; I just dropped in twopence. You were noble-hearted, I was callous and mercenary. But, by God, if we'd asked the old chap to choose between us I doubt if he'd have chosen you. We're all humbugs, Charlie; it comes so natural to us, it seems damned odd you should have to work so hard at it. No hard feelings, Charlie," he called, as Forbes stalked across the room and left.

"Sorry," said Todd, grinning at his chief. "I've been wanting to say that to Charlie for years. But I suppose I shouldn't have said it here."

"He means well, William, particularly as regards Curdie."

Todd laughed. "Now normally I wouldn't send a dead dog to Towellan for a holiday, but it might almost be worth while going there myself, just to watch the fun. Talk about the cuckoo in the nest!"

"Well, William," asked the headmaster, "do you want me to send for the rest of these boys?"

"Yes, certainly. We must be impartial. But Curdie's the culprit."

"I'm afraid I'm like Charlie, I'm not at all convinced. The boy seemed to me to answer very candidly."

Todd shook his head at such credulity.

CHAPTER
SIX

At the bus-stop Gillian and Alistair were waiting in freckled excitement to inform him, before he was on the pavement, that their grandmother had arrived while he was out, she was in the house now, and she was going with them to Towellan tomorrow.

This news so disconcerted him he forgot to introduce Tom.

"But she said she couldn't go this year," he said, as if they were to blame.

"Yes, but she's able now," replied Gillian, who kept glancing aside at Tom. "She said she'd managed to get Mr Treel to take his holidays later."

"She'd bully him into it," muttered Forbes.

Treel was the manager of Mrs Storrocks's large furniture shop in Hamilton.

"What about *him*, Daddy?" whispered Gillian.

"Good gracious, yes." Forbes halted. "How silly of me. I forgot you've never met. Well, children, this is Tom Curdie."

He felt proud of Tom: that morning had seen a transformation; a bath and some new clothes had turned him into a boy that even Todd must have approved.

Fair-haired Alistair, in many ways so like his mother, shook hands with a cheerful squirm of embarrassment. But Gillian, dark-haired, dark-eyed idealist, was aggressive in her curiosity. She did not offer her hand; she merely gave a quick nod and a smile; but her eyes, in their nests of freckles, were as sharp as beaks.

"I'm Gillian Forbes," she said.

Her father laughed. "I've just told him that," he said.

"I wanted to tell him myself."

Her father didn't quite understand. He would have to keep an eye on Gillian and make sure she didn't tease the poor lad. There was a little streak of her Grandmother Storrocks in Gillian, though it was true, as Mary often said, that she was mostly a Forbes.

As they walked on Alistair carried Tom's small case, but it was Gillian who walked by his side.

"Can you row?" she asked.

"A wee bit."

"Where did you learn?"

"Rouken Glen."

"That's not the sea."

Though he smiled, Tom knew he would have to watch carefully this girl in the blue dress and with the blue, fiercely inquisitive eyes. She would try to worry all his secrets out of him.

"Can you swim?" she asked.

"Only three strokes."

"Then you can't swim."

Her father intervened tactfully. "Tom hasn't had your opportunities, Gillian."

"I just wanted to find out what he can do," she replied, blandly. "If he wants to learn to row and swim, I'm willing to teach him."

"That's kind of you, Gillian."

"Some hopes!" said Alistair, a victim of his sister's tuition.

Gillian returned to Tom. "Do you know anything about wild flowers?"

"Not much."

"Can you name ten?" She held up all her fingers.

"No."

"Five?" She dropped one hand.

"Just three."

"What three?"

"Daisies, buttercups, dandelions."

She was about to smile at such a silly answer, when she suddenly suspected irony. Was he laughing at her? Though she looked hard she could not say for certain.

"When we're at Towellan, Gillian," said her father, "you'll take Tom out and show him all the wild flowers you know."

"Yes, Daddy."

Then she retreated into a silence as deep as Tom's.

At his gate Forbes paused to inspect his protégé. Outwardly all seemed passable, but was the dark quiet hair really depopulated? Into his mind jumped the absurd name that the English Royalists, in elegant satire, had given to lice: Covenanters. So at his gate, with his children waiting, and with his wife watching from the window, and with neighbours watching from theirs, Forbes, seeing a small boy's hair, saw also lonely moors where men had been killed for their faith and where whaups now flew about their memorials. It was not altogether irrelevant. Seated at this moment in his own armchair was one who, had she lived in the seventeenth century, would have justified the murder of an archbishop with a text from the Old Testament.

Living in the twentieth century Mrs Storrocks shared its prejudices. To her Jews were the wolves of business that devoured the profits she ought to make. Communists were anti-Christ; but she did not accept the corollary that Americans were pro-Christ; these, principally for their gum-chewing, their actresses' breasts, and their men's haircuts, she distrusted. South Africa, she believed, would never be a happy country until all the blacks were exterminated; but she was also convinced that its leaders ought to be exterminated too, for wanting to be republicans. Above all, however, she had been prejudiced against Charlie; right from the beginning she had regarded him as a poor match for her only child. His youthful ideals, those white does skimming through the greenness of his marriage, had found in her an insatiable tigress. Now here he was, in his unsuccessful middle-age, leading home another such doe.

In the tiny living-room Mrs Storrocks sat facing the door. Her hat, like a blue helmet with white plume, was square upon her head. Two rings glittered on her fingers; a necklace of blue stones sparkled; blue earrings twinkled; but her eyes resolutely gave forth no light. She had always been a handsome woman, with healthy pink complexion and well-fed robustness. Now the whiteness of her hair gave to the tightness of her lips a matriarchal assurance; this was assisted by her thousands in the bank and her certainty of heaven.

Mary, often his ally against her mother, was in this present contest unreliable. She wore an apron and had been cooking the lunch. When Tom was presented to her she stood in silence for a second or two, looking like her mother as she made swift calculations, which involved human affections, however, and not sums of money. Then she took the boy's hand and gave him her friendliest smile, which, as Charlie often boasted, would civilise headhunters.

"So you're Tom Curdie?" she said. "I've heard a lot about you. I hope you'll be happy with us, Tom."

Her glances, maternal in their sympathy, were no less so in their vigilance, as they took in his ears, neck, and hair.

"Thanks, Mrs Forbes," he murmured, and faintly blushed.

"Well, lunch is ready," she said. "Alistair, will you take Tom up and let him see where to wash his hands?"

Alistair eagerly agreed: it was a step towards eating, and besides, he felt sorry for the strange boy. Both went out.

There was silence until the bathroom door upstairs was heard closing.

"Well, Mary, not such a monster after all?" said Charlie.

She had to smile. "He seems a nice enough little boy. What about his hair, though?"

"Attended to."

"By whom? I thought his mother was a slut who couldn't keep her own head clean."

"You'll find his hair all right."

"You will, Charlie. I'm leaving that part of it to you."

"Very good."

"I don't think I'm going to like him." It was Gillian who spoke. "He never says what he's thinking. He's laughing at us all the time."

"Hold your tongue, miss," cried her father. "If you can't find anything hospitable to say, please have the charity to say nothing. And don't try to be smart at somebody else's expense."

His wife thought that that smartness was really an attempt to copy him.

"Be quiet, Charlie," she said. "She's just a child."

"So is he."

"Children are seldom fair to each other."

"Yes, children who know each other, Mary. But this boy's hardly five minutes in the house."

"I'm sorry," said Gillian.

Her father stared at her with fondness flooding his large, sad face. "So am I, Gillian. Our nerves are all strained. We need our holiday."

"Your nerves must be very bad indeed, Charles," said his mother-in-law, "seeing they've prevented you from saying you're glad to see me."

"That goes without saying, Mrs Storrocks."

"Still, I like to hear it. The weather looks settled, Charles, so I thought I'd join you at Towellan for a week or two. That's to say, if there are no objections."

"We'll be delighted to have you with us, Mrs Storrocks."

He spoke cordially. After all, she was the owner of the cottage at Towellan. The cousin who usually lived in it rented it from her.

"Mary's been telling me about this boy you're taking with you."

He waited, but instead of snarling she smiled.

"It might turn out to be a sound idea," she said. "If it doesn't help you in your career, I don't see how it can hinder you."

"It's for the boy's own sake, Mrs Storrocks."

Mary shook her head at him: the signal meant that now, just when she was about to serve lunch, wasn't the time to instruct her mother as to his true motive.

Mrs Storrocks seemed satisfied. She rose as the two boys returned to the living-room.

"I want you, boy," she said to Tom, "to sit beside me and tell me all about yourself."

"Yes, ma'am," he replied, though what he meant to tell her was no more than what she already knew.

"No, mother," said Mrs Forbes. "I've set his place between Gillian and Alistair."

Her husband looked at her in gratitude.

CHAPTER
SEVEN

The taxi took them right into the crowded station, close to the platform at which their train was waiting. Unfortunately, when Forbes came back from paying the driver it was to learn that Alistair, whom excitement always affected in that way, needed to go to the lavatory. His mother and grandmother were scolding him for such inopportuneness.

To be setting out on holiday was to have left blame behind. Forbes remembered that he, too, as a boy had had that weakness, if indeed it was a weakness. Rocks did not have their insides stirred by anticipations of joy and loveliness.

"Plenty of time," he said calmly. "The train doesn't leave for another quarter of an hour."

"We happen to want seats," said Mrs Storrocks, "and there are thousands pouring in."

Though she exaggerated, it was true that many people were going for their train. All the seats might well be taken. Nevertheless, he would not be panicked into being cross; instead, he stroked Alistair's head.

"Off you go, son," he said. "We'll wait."

"But we'll not get seats," cried Alistair.

"Never mind about that. Just you go and make yourself comfortable."

"You'd better go with him," said Mary. "He'll get lost in this crowd."

"Certainly. Come on, Alistair."

"You go too, Tom," said Mary. "And give us our tickets, Charlie. We'll try to keep your seats."

"Very good, dear." He handed over the tickets.

"Hurry, please," pleaded Alistair.

"You should have gone before you left the house," whispered Gillian.

"I did, twice."

Frowning, she sought an answer to that. "Baby," she said.

"My tea was too hot," he protested.

Then off he had to race, to keep up with his father. Tom Curdie raced too. Many people, clumsy with heavy cases, staggered into them on the way to the Gourock train. Bound for that same train, Forbes chuckled at thus heading in the opposite direction; it was Columbus-like daring.

He halted at the top of the lavatory steps.

"There's no need for me to go down," he said. "I'll wait here. Got a penny?"

"Sure, pop." Alistair had been holding on to it like a talisman.

"Go with him, Tom. Speed's the thing. But don't panic."

But as soon as they had vanished impatience like a dog came to sniff and then snarl at his heels. He could not keep his eyes off the big clock. Every engine that screamed he was sure was the one pulling the Gourock train; it was warning him it was ready to be off. He began to think the boys must be dawdling, but in fairness he reminded himself of the delays encountered in the mechanics of modern relief: locks jammed, buttons were intractable. Fear made him foolish: he envied gulls that defecated flying, and he saw the limitations of being human. Proof came suddenly; his own bowels heaved. "Good God," he muttered. Though he smiled, as he must at the triviality of his predicament, there was no quelling that riot within. At forty-nine he was being attacked by a weakness of boyhood. Was not adult life a series of such ambushes from the past?

As the boys panted up, he went racing down. They were astonished.

"Wait here. Won't be a minute."

And he was hardly a minute. In and out of that cubicle he rushed, galloped upstairs, seized the boys, and raced for the train.

Gillian's head stuck out of a compartment. She called to them.

Drenched with triumph, he pushed the boys in and then entered himself. He sat down not noticing his wife's embarrassment at her mother's brazenness in reserving that seat for him.

"What in heaven's name kept you?" she whispered.

"No hurry, dear," he said, beaming. "Look, there's the train just started."

The compartment was stuffy and overcrowded.

"We should," said Mrs Storrocks loudly, "have travelled first-class. I'm willing to pay for a little comfort."

The strangers might have felt insulted; instead, they tried to make a little more room for her.

"A' the same," said one of them, a pleasant-faced woman, "the difference in price is ridiculous."

"There should be only one class nowadays," said a thin man with a moustache.

"Third-class folk," said another woman shyly, "are far cheerier."

Forbes was still beaming. But his mother-in-law had not intended to provoke friendliness.

"I like room to breathe," she said.

"You'll get it doon the watter," said a fat woman in a corner, and she began to laugh so jollily that Forbes pictured her paddling in the sea, with her skirts held gallusly high, revealing legs as thick and barnacled as the legs of Towellan pier.

Kindness prevailed. A man took Tom Curdie on his knee. Forbes dandled Alistair. Most of the room gained was given to Mrs Storrocks, who was satisfied.

In time they passed Dumbarton Rock, serene in sunshine. Forbes pointed to it.

"A famous chunk of Scotland," he said, and next minute, with greater enthusiasm, was pointing to a more distant still huger chunk: Ben Lomond.

"You'll be a teacher, maybe," said the shy woman.

He admitted what he knew others would have falsely denied. Todd on holiday always pretended he was the owner of a flourishing butcher's business. To live in a hotel, he said, and be known as a teacher, was to suffer the worst humiliation known to man. Even the beer bottles in the bar leered at you.

"Yes, he's a teacher," said Mrs Storrocks, "and this poor lad here is one of his pupils. He's from a slum home, and wouldn't be getting a holiday at all if it wasn't for my son-in-law's kindness."

As she spoke she gazed with insinuation at those members of the Glasgow public, those ratepayers and voters, those choosers of councillors. Mary's nudge she ignored. As for her son-in-law's little moan, she didn't hear it.

The ratepayers extolled Forbes and pitied Tom. One woman took a half-crown from her purse and handed it to the boy.

He glanced towards his benefactor for guidance; none was there.

"Go on, son," said the woman, "take it. A holiday at the seaside is gey expensive these days."

He took it, with politest thanks.

Two other gifts were made. These he similarly accepted.

They were passing Port Glasgow. In a breakers' yard lay the skeleton of a great ship. At this, rather than at the spacious Firth, Forbes gazed.

"Well, it's a grand morning for the sail," said Mrs Storrocks.

There were murmurs of agreement from all, with one exception. Forbes saw what they did: the children splashing in Cardwell Bay; the many yachts, with sails of different colours; the steamers at the pier; and across the Firth the craggy Argyll hills pierced by sea-lochs; but disenchanting all that, was his own unworthiness.

Malice, as well as honesty, could uncover truth. What Mrs Storrocks had hinted others already had hinted; Todd had bluntly stated it; and it was partly true. Without doubt, at the very back of his mind from the very beginning had been the hope that his befriending of this slum delinquent child might reach the ears of authority. He had dreamed that at some future promotion interview some favourable councillor, briefed beforehand, would ask: "Is it the case, Mr Forbes, that you have taken a slum pupil with you during your holidays, with your own family? Now why did you?" His answer would be modest but effective. These considerations had been in his mind, camouflaged like grouse in heather; now Mrs Storrocks had set them flying.

The danger lay in falling into resentment against Tom Curdie, in seeing the boy's admirable reticence as some kind of sinister senile composure, such as was shown by the changeling of Highland legend, that creature introduced by the malevolent folk of the other world into a man's home, to pollute the joy and faith of family.

As he walked out of the station on to the pier, with the Firth sparkling before him, and saw on the steamers' destination boards those magical names, Kilcreggan, Craigendoran, Tighnabruaich, Largs, Millport, and Rothesay, he knew that if he was a charlatan the magic would not work for him.

The *St Columba* had left the pier and was heading across for Argyll when Forbes, in the breezy bow, where he always preferred to stand (being protected by his fat, was Mary's joke), found Tom suddenly by his side. He should, he knew, have rejoiced at this first opportunity to introduce the boy from the squalid slum to all this cleansing and liberating beauty: the Holy Loch, so called, it was said, because many hundreds of years ago a ship carrying earth from the Holy Land had been wrecked in it; Loch Long, at the head of which was the famous hill called The Cobbler; Hunter's Quay, haven of yachts; the Cloch Lighthouse; Dunroth, steepled and smoking below its green hills; the islands, Bute, the two Cumbraes, and Arran, with its wonderful skyline. "Here it is," he should have been able to cry, "our heritage, Tom, yours and mine, because we are Scottish; and what we see now is only the promise of vaster riches. In no other country in the world, not even in fabled Greece, is there loveliness so various and so inspiring in so small a space. Here is the antidote to Donaldson's Court; here is the guarantee of that splendid and courageous manhood to which every Scots boy is entitled by birth." All this should he have spoken as the spray swept up from the bows with the exhilaration of singing, and the seagulls glided overhead with their feet tucked so delicately under their tails, and their golden eyes questing. But a voice, like Todd's, as insistent as the engines, kept shouting: "Guff, Charlie; admit it's a lot of guff."

"Mr Forbes, sir," said Tom.

"Well?"

The boy paused and gazed over the water in which sun-sparkles swam like fabulous swans. He seemed to be making a final decision. Then he held out his right hand, closed. Slowly he opened it to reveal, like the eggs of those birds of glory, three silver coins. They were the gifts from the people in the train.

"What will I do with these, sir?"

"What do you mean?"

"I shouldn't have taken them. That's why you're angry with me, isn't it?"

Luckily, there at the forefront of the steamer, even on such a sunny morning, was too cool for most passengers. The only others near were a party from Lancashire, who were enjoying themselves too loudly to want to overhear anybody else's conversation.

Forbes therefore was able to concentrate on finding some adequate way to apologies.

"I am not angry with you, Tom," he said.

"I thought you were, sir, in the train."

"Not with you, Tom."

"But I took these."

"Why not? They were offered in kindness, with no thought of any return. Never snub true kindness."

"I want you to take them, sir."

"Do you mean, to keep for you?"

Tom hesitated, touching his new jerkin. "No, sir. To help to pay for these clothes."

Then hilarity burst out around them. A seagull had dropped its dirt upon the hat of a small, shrill, light-hearted, large-nosed woman among the Lancashire folk. In pretended rage she besought her uproarious friends to point out to her the culprit among the dozen or so flying above; she would report it to the captain. They informed her with hearty humour; many fingers pointed to many gulls.

Forbes felt then not only glad but shriven; he was able to love gulls and people again.

"Thanks all the same, Tom," he said. "It's a fine thing to pay one's debts. But what you owe me is no debt. At any rate let us keep money out of it. We are inclined, I'm afraid, to be rather a mercenary people."

As he spoke the steamer was drawing in to Dunroth pier, where loudspeakers were blaring out "Ye Banks and Braes o' Bonnie Doon".

"Enrich your mind, Tom," he went on. "Never let yourself be stampeded into the great grab for money."

"No, sir."

"Mind you, don't agree just because I'm your teacher. I'm afraid in many things we teachers are fallible." Then he heard Todd's voice again: "Don't be a bloody traitor, Charlie. They find us out soon enough. For God's sake don't help them."

He watched the people streaming happily down the gangways on to the pier. Their pockets would be laden with hoarded money; most of their happiness would consist in spending it. Glasgow folk, a coast landlady had once told him, were the ones to splash the siller; East Coasters and the English were far cannier. A Glasgow man himself, he had felt proud of that holiday liberality; but now, from his eyrie of truth, he saw that it was perhaps another aspect of their worship of money: earning and spending, they served their deity well.

But that black belief could not possess his mind forever; out it had to go, or rather into some deep dark hole in his subconscious it had to plunge, when the steamer began to leave Dunroth pier, with Towellan next stop. Bells clanged, hawsers were slipped off iron capstans and heaved into water that bubbled like lemonade, people waved, children cheered, gulls wailed, and the loudspeakers bawled "The Road to the Isles". Still in his eyrie, Forbes gazed ahead towards Towellan, now drawing close. Yonder was the little pier, with the lighthouse beyond, and beyond that again the magnificent skyline of the Arran hills, forming the Sleeping Warrior.

He put his hand on Tom's shoulder and pressed so hard it hurt; it somehow had to hurt, for it was a kind of initiation.

"Look, Tom," he said, "the hills of Arran!"

"Yes, sir."

But that was too cautious, too subdued a reply.

"The hills of Arran!" repeated Forbes, in exaltation. "Can you see the 'Sleeping Warrior'?"

Tom shook his head.

This was indeed initiation; once it had been Gillian, then Alistair, and now Tom Curdie.

"It's the jagged skyline, Tom. It looks like a helmeted warrior lying on his back. Can you make him out?"

"I think so, sir."

"Cherish that vision, Tom; it will sustain you in times of trouble."

A gull flew past; its eye gleamed like Todd's.

Then Gillian and Alistair, who had been running all over the steamer, arrived panting to say their mother and grandmother were waiting below.

Forbes put his arm round Tom's neck.

"This is Towellan, Tom," he said. "We have arrived. You cannot see our cottage yet, for it's round the point, but this is the place where you will be living for the next week or two. As you can see, it is very beautiful. You will fish, like those boys; you will row a boat, like those others; you will roam over those green hills."

"Mummy said you'd to hurry," said Gillian.

He held Tom's hand as they went down the stairs; but he let it go when he saw Mary gaze oddly at that clasp.

The two ladies had had a cup of tea in peace; they were refreshed and in good humour.

"Where have you two been all the time?" asked Mary.

"On the bridge, like captains. Weren't we, Tom?"

Tom nodded and smiled. Mary thought she detected in the smile amusement at her husband's extravagance; she pardoned it for she also thought she saw affection, rather touching on so guarded and precocious a face.

Forbes took out his tickets and publicly tore them in half: it was a symbolical act; the journey was completed, the haven reached.

Mary stretched forward to look at the halves he was holding.

"I hope you've got the right halves ready."

"Now, Mary!"

"Well, last year didn't the man have to shout you back?"

He grinned and scratched his ear with those half-tickets before he risked looking at them. They were, he saw triumphantly, the right ones: it was a good omen.

CHAPTER
EIGHT

He was like an exile returning: not one who had made a vulgar fortune during his stay abroad, but one who had come back rich only in love. Bob Moodie, the pierman, was slow, canny, but cordial in taking the hand Charlie offered so enthusiastically. Bob's own hand, sunburnt and leathery, had to be brought out of the money satchel in which he gathered the twopenny tolls. That he still took from Charlie the full amount was of course no reflection on the sincerity of his welcome. It was not his pier, he could not confer the freedom of it upon his friends; but as he had been living in Towellan for over fifty years the village in a profound way did belong to him, and its freedom he conferred, with characteristic canniness. Aye, the fishing wasn't at all bad this year; the clegs, though, were wicked, the worst he could mind; and the rabbits just weren't rabbits any more, they were now "myxes", creatures with bulging eyes and heads.

Despite his sympathy for rabbits, Bob was as inquisitive as any hungry weasel.

"That's a stranger, surely," he said, nodding towards Tom.

"Yes, Bob. A pupil." Then he added what he should not, though it was evoked by the trust of friendship. "Comes from a slum district. I thought he needed a tonic like Towellan. Very clever boy."

"He looks it. Not much'll go past that one. But is that your guid-mither giving you the wave? She's getting impatient."

Bob grinned at his understatement: Mrs Storrocks he considered an impudent old bitch. Once, with the pier crowded, she had upbraided him because of his twopence toll on and off.

Charlie hurried off the pier.

"I hope you don't think, Charles," said Mrs Storrocks, "that because you talk to them here they're your friends."

"That's Charlie's business, Mother," said Mary.

"The people here are all small-minded," went on Mrs Storrocks. "They spend their time running each other down. They've got little else to do. Don't trust them. I hope you said nothing to that loudmouth about the boy there?"

"Of course he didn't," snapped Mary. "Why should he?"

Charlie thought it better not to tell: they did not seem to understand.

Outside the pier a tinker was swaggering up and down playing the bagpipe, while his wife, tanned and taciturn as an Indian squaw, padded about with his cap held out. Mrs Storrocks, who disapproved of tinkers, dropped nothing in; Mary put in two pennies; the three children a penny each; and Charlie a shilling, causing his mother-in-law to snort and mutter about a fool and his money being easily parted.

There was another extravagance she did not condemn. In the space outside the pier stood Towellan's last landau, black and polished, with high, red-spoked wheels and red upholstery. In her heart Mrs Storrocks loved travelling in it; up there, rolling along in dignity, she felt what she knew she was, a lady.

Its owner was old Willie McPhunn. In the days when motorcars were scarce here in inaccessible Argyll, he had plied between Towellan and Dunroth, four miles along the coast. Nowadays he was content to drive visitors to and from the pier, and to take them drives along the sea-road. In his hey-day he had had tall fine-legged well-matched horses; now he was reduced to two sturdy ponies that worked on a farm.

Willie wasn't to be seen. The ponies cropped the warm grass, as if a whole day's leisure was in front of them. They were in the charge of a small fair-haired boy in a kilt.

"Well," said Charlie, "why don't we get aboard? It's as cheap sitting as standing."

"I'll hold the horses, mister," said the kilted ostler.

"Yes, you do that, sonny."

Gillian and Alistair had to be restrained from leaping up immediately.

"What if they bolt?" asked Mary.

"Och, I think I can handle 'em," said Charlie, laughing.

"Maybe it'd be better if you went and looked for Willie."

"I'll tell you where to find him," said Mrs Storrocks, scowling in the direction of the hotel bar.

"He'll be here in a minute," said Charlie. "Right, Tom, we'll give you the honour of being first."

Tom ascended with a grin that made Mary feel he was not after all going to be as awkward a guest as she had feared. Gillian and Alistair came next, squabbling for precedence; then Mary, helped by her husband; and then Mrs Storrocks, insisting on managing unaided, and giving a fine imitation of a drunk duchess whose every failure made her next attempt still more dignified.

"All aboard?" cried Charlie. "Good." And with lucky agility he sprang into the driver's seat.

There he saw at his feet Willie's top-hat and trumpet; the former he wore, the latter he blew, if his passengers were intelligent enough to wish it.

Charlie picked up the hat.

"Don't you dare," whispered Mary, laughing.

"Why not?" Suddenly he clapped on the hat, and snatching up the trumpet put it to his lips and blew, not very musically but loudly enough to startle gulls and people down on the shore, and to make the two ponies raise their heads in doubt. Thus, with the *St Columba*'s three red funnels disappearing round the lighthouse promontory, Charlie sounded his defiance: here he was arrived in his kingdom, where regret, humiliation, mercenariness, and failure did not exist.

When he turned round he saw Tom Curdie gazing at him with a wonder like a transparence, through which could surely be glimpsed, fugitive as minnows in a pool, gleams of astonished affection.

80

"Have you taken leave of your senses, Charles?" gasped his mother-in-law.

His wife's rebuke was mild. "We're conspicuous enough, Charlie."

It was true, several people were watching and laughing. With a flourish Charlie took off the hat.

"Let me blow it, pop," asked Alistair, reaching out for the trumpet.

"If you do, Alistair Forbes," said his grandmother, "not a penny do you get from me all this holiday. I don't pay people to make a fool of me." She turned on her son-in-law. "Remember who we've got with us," she whispered. "What's he going to tell the others when he goes back? What respect are you going to get? You'll not be able to show your face."

Her words proved she did not understand. Charlie winked at Tom, in whose mind that blowing of the trumpet had opened the first small window.

"Well, it's done one thing anyway," said Mary. "It's brought Willie."

The old man came hurrying, or at least trying to hurry. His legs were so thin and shaky that the gaiters he wore as a kind of livery to go with the top-hat looked like supports. He was so stooped that at every step he seemed about to scrape from his boots the dried cow dung on them.

"Drunk," muttered Mrs Storrocks, but not even she believed it.

Charlie was horrified. In his recollection this old man had been immortal; the lighthouse itself might have been expected to totter sooner than Willie. Yet now those very whiskers, once so brawny with beer, wilted.

His wits and friendliness were soon shown to be as lively as ever. He had a joke for each one, even for Mrs Storrocks; for Tom Curdie, the stranger, he had a special handshake.

"You'll be a cousin of Alistair's?" he asked.

"Nothing of the kind," snapped Mrs Storrocks. "He's no relation. He's a scholar of Mr Forbes's; just that."

Willie winked at Tom. "Just that, eh? Weel, I'm sure that's a grand thing to be."

"Thanks, Willie," said Charlie.

With a wave of his hand to the little boy in the kilt Willie set the ponies going.

"Sorry I had to keep you waiting, Mr Forbes," he said.

"Charlie's the name, Willie."

"Where I was your name was mentioned. Maybe you'll no' mind of wee Eddie Tulloch, wha used to be roadman years back?"

"No, I can't say I do."

"A wee man, but no cantankerous wi it. Ye'll hae noticed how wee men are often a shade cantankerous. Never wee Eddie. An awfu' sweet nature for a man. Not braw, though. He would say himself his shovel was a better-looking shovel than he was a man. But his he'rt was bonny."

"You say he mentioned me?"

"Aye, that he did. It seems, years ago, when he was working round by Loch Striven, he met you once. You were on a picnic and asked him to take a drop of tea wi you."

"Yes, I remember," cried Charlie. "A tiny man with a sharp face?"

"It's sharper noo. Something happened this winter past that was like a whetstane to his face. Jean his wife dee'd."

"I'm sorry to hear that," said Charlie, and he was sorry not only for the little roadman's sake. Though he had blown the trumpet in Towellan, death and grief and decay were here.

"He'll no be long ahint her," said Willie.

"And he remembered our picnic?" asked Charlie, in wonder. "It must have been at least eight years ago."

"The tea was still sweet in his mooth."

Never had the Firth looked so beautiful. The roadsides were gardens of honeysuckle and wild white roses. So simple those wild roses, so spare, so austere, with their five petals, their untamed bushes, and their thorns as sharp as a wild cat's claws, they symbolised for Charlie his country's sad harsh history, enacted against a background of magnificent loveliness. Their petals were as soft as silk. Many times must little Eddie Tulloch the roadman have sat down to drink his tea and eat his bread and cheese beside them. Yes, a wild white rose was the badge for Tom Curdie to wear in Towellan.

They passed the Lion-rock, and there, with its lawn in front as big as a field, shone the cottage, white-washed walls and blue-painted woodwork. Behind rose the wood with its green glades of grass and lichened rock and ferns, where last year rabbits had played. Beyond the drystone dyke soared the hills. It was all familiar and beloved, and yet it was strange, too, full of hints of thresholds leading into another world where the beauty of the wild rose did sustain like food.

The chimney was smoking, and Mrs McDonald, her hair as white as the house, was standing outside to welcome them. She lived along the road and every summer received them thus, with friendship the only payment. She would have a meal ready, better than any to be had in the dearest hotel in Dunroth; there would be her own baking, with a special jelly made from rowanberries and Towellan apples.

While she was shaking hands with them all she seemed to Charlie to represent some goddess chosen to preside at this consummation, after all the other tutelary spirits, such as the engine-driver, the steamer captain, and Willie the coachman had done their parts and gone. They were all present again in her.

During the bustle Charlie slipped out to the garden at the back of the house. He stood amidst rhododendrons, so that he would not be seen. There he gazed at the wood in which the "cushie-doos" were moaning. In some way he had to express his homage and thankfulness. Once, while at the University, he had seen three Moslem students, in a public street, salaam towards Mecca, thousands of miles away; but for his purpose salaaming would be grotesque. Saluting would be too military; blowing kisses too effeminate; stretching out of hands, like a lover, too ostentatious. The only way seemed to be by just standing still, as if he was another bush or tree, so that even the sparrows marauding among the gooseberries, were not disturbed. When he breathed "Thank God", he was sure so were all the other presences he could see, trees and bushes and flowers and birds, breathing a similar thankfulness.

Then Gillian shouted from an upstairs window. "Daddy, you've to come at once. Dinner's being served."

He turned to wave at her, and suddenly caught sight of Tom Curdie's pale face lurking amid the ramblers that covered the trellis-work at the side of the house.

"Well, Tom," he cried, "what do you think of it?"

"I like it, sir."

The words were commonplace, but they were uttered with such a quiet earnestness that surely they meant commitment. Charlie realised it was the first time he had heard the boy commit himself to anything.

"Very much," added Tom.

"You couldn't help liking it, Tom," cried Charlie, in glee. "I knew it."

Again Gillian shouted. "Last call, Daddy."

"We'd better do as we're told, Tom," said Charlie, laughing. "Let's go in."

With his arm round the boy's neck they went in, looking so much like father and son that as Mary saw them she couldn't help feeling jealous on behalf of her own son Alistair. It seemed to her that this mysterious boy Curdie would have to be watched carefully, otherwise he would without compunction steal what belonged to Alistair and Gillian. If ever there was a man able to be duped by a show of affection and gratitude it

85

was Charlie, especially here in Towellan where he would buy white heather off a tinker-wife, although he himself knew at least three places on the hills around where it grew.

But she said nothing, and made Tom especially welcome at the table. His portions were larger than Alistair's, for after all he was older and had more need of food.

CHAPTER
NINE

Like a squire carrying his knight's shield, was Charlie's verdict; like a dog with the sense to lick the hand that fed it, was Mrs Storrocks's. Both were describing Tom Curdie that first day at Towellan.

Eager to supply the family with their first sea-fresh cod or whiting, Charlie in the secrecy of early morning, before breakfast, set off on the old bicycle with the buckled wheels to the sandy nook a mile or so away, where spoutfish abounded for those with the knowledge and skill to catch them. He had calculated that the tide would just be right.

He carried a pail over his shoulder and a spade across his handlebars. Dressed in mauve corduroy shorts, leather moccasins, and white open-necked shirt that revealed the hairiness of his broad chest, he sang as he zig-zagged in the sunshine along the lonely road by the sea. Not a car, not a human being, not a sheep, not a rabbit did he meet; only a frog which he wished good-morning.

Arrived at the bay, he pulled off his moccasins, rolled up his shorts, and waded into the glittering water, searching for the tell-tale holes in the sand. Within a couple of minutes he had caught a spoutfish, a beauty, with its shell almost a foot long: it was bait to boast about, whatever fish it caught. Held in his hand it became a wand: the whole scene became one of enchantment; himself alone save for some oyster-catchers, a ship far out on the Firth, and the hills on every horizon save the sea's receding into a blue legendary remoteness.

He could not keep his imagination from playing: now, knee-deep in the water, with his dripping pail in one hand and the spade in the other, he was Crusoe, castaway for twenty years, gazing out over the companionless ocean; now, crouched, so that the sea's ripples kissed his bottom, he was an ancient Caledonian, watching the coracle from Ireland with the men of God; and now, upright, with the spade levelled like a sword, he prepared to resist the landing of Redcoats from an English man-o'-war, whose sails were represented by a white cloud. In the intervals between these rôles he delved in the sand for spoutfish, finding them with a luckiness that more than the sunshine and the silence and the beauty of the scene gave him in his own self as Charlie Forbes a continuing sense of enchantment. There had been mornings when he had returned with not one spoutfish; this morning he would go back with a pailful. Surely it meant that the Towellan benison, in which he believed and at which such as Todd scoffed, was this summer at work in its full potency.

Trivial accidents were to be smiled at. His feet grew cold and numb. Stepping clumsily over a rock, he slipped on seaweed, clutched at sunlight, reeled, and sat down with a splash in about a foot of water. Even on dry land his corpulent rising from a sitting to a standing position was never instantaneous; here, in the sea, with a pailful of spoutfish in one hand and a spade in the other, and with his fundament chilled, ascension was much slower, and far less graceful than Aphrodite's. But up he got at last, laughing, and walked dripping to the shore. His white city legs were now almost blue, as if stained with woad, and his shorts had undergone a sea-change to imperial purple; his shirt too was splashed, and his face was sprinkled with silver drops.

He was ankle-deep when he noticed that he was not alone after all. Near the boulder on which the moccasins lay sat Tom Curdie; but he did not look quite human, he was almost the changeling again. Otherwise, why no laughter, no smile even, no grimace of amusement, only this intense antagonistic contemplativeness, suitable for confronting the accumulated injustices of mankind, hardly for witnessing a fat teacher's frolics in the sunlit sea.

Gingerly on the pebbles, Charlie approached him.

"Hello, how long have you been here?"

"About half an hour, sir."

So he had seen Crusoe, the ancient Caledonian, and the intrepid Jacobite, as well as the splashing clown?

"I slipped," said Charlie, laughing and slapping his soaked bottom.

"Yes, sir. Did you hurt yourself?"

"No, no. Why in heaven's name didn't you laugh? The seagulls did. Why didn't you? I hope it wasn't because you didn't want me to know you were here?"

"No, sir."

"You should have let me know. It's not quite mannerly to sit and watch someone in silence. But you must learn to laugh. I don't think, Tom, I've ever heard you laugh. Now if it'd been you who had tumbled into the sea and got your behind wet, I'd have laughed. Such laughter isn't malicious, you know; it's all part of the fun. Now what do you think of my spoutfish?" He took one out and, proud as Neptune, held it up.

Tom had never seen one before. He gazed at it in such a way as to delight its catcher.

Charlie pretended to shave his cheek with it.

"Also known as razor-fish," he cried; but his hand was now shaking so much that if it had been a real razor he would have slashed himself. So were his teeth chattering.

"I'm afraid I'll have to dash back and get changed," he said.

He hurried into his moccasins. When he was about to mount the bicycle he turned to the boy, who still watched him with keen enigmatic attention.

"What about you?" asked Charlie. "I'm afraid I can't risk you on the bar. This bike's liable to fall to pieces."

"It's all right, sir. I'll walk."

"You won't have had your breakfast yet?"

"No, sir."

"Why did you come?"

"I always get up early, sir. When I saw you leaving the house I thought it would be all right if I followed you. I knew you were going for bait."

Charlie was delighted by that long answer. "You should have given me a shout," he said. "Did you sleep all right in the hut?"

It was in the garden at the back, comfortable enough and weatherproof; but it had meant segregation and Charlie hadn't been pleased. Mary had convinced him it was the only sensible arrangement.

"Oh yes, sir, I slept fine."

"The owls didn't frighten you?"

"No." He said it as though on the contrary he'd lain and listened to them in wonder. "If you like, sir, I'll carry your spade."

"No, thanks. I'll manage. Don't be long. Breakfast will be waiting for you."

When Charlie, at a bend in the road, turned his head he saw that Tom had already begun to run, not in any fright or sulk at being left alone, but with a quiet, almost happy determination.

"Good," said Charlie, "very good. But all the same, if you're going to follow me about like a squire his knight in armour, well, it might make things a bit awkward. I'll have to make sure you play with Alistair and Gillian. That's what you're here for, after all, to find your childhood."

That first long halcyon morning was spent in taking the spoutfish out of their shells, swimming, investigating sea-pools, playing cricket on the lawn, and erecting the swing on the oak tree behind the house. Tom took part in everything, in such a fair-minded, helpful way as to show up the quarrelsome and selfish attitude of Alistair who claimed the most spoutfish, the first innings, and the first swing, and of Gillian who combated those claims. Mrs Storrocks defended her grandchildren: it was the nature of healthy normal children to squabble at their games. Charlie was indignant at such partiality; several times he reproved his own children by pointing to the example of Tom, until Mary quietly told him to stop it, otherwise he'd turn them against Tom.

After lunch Charlie proposed a visit to the ruined castle about a mile from the house. The path to it was grassy and not too steep. Once Mrs Storrocks had reached it, and in spite of clegs and Charlie's raptures, she had approved of the view. This time she declined: she would sit in the garden and read. Mary too decided it would be too energetic for her so early in the holiday, on such a warm day; she would sit with her mother.

Before the expedition set forth, laden with lemonade, biscuits and sweets, Mary took Charlie aside and reminded him that Alistair was only ten, and must not be led into exploits too arduous for him; he must also not be made to feel that because of his comparative lack of strength he was a nuisance to the others. He was, she said, very sensitive about being outdone; and though tempted, she said no more, although Charlie's boisterous assurances showed her he hadn't taken her hints. She managed before they left to speak to Gillian, whom she found much sharper.

"He's sucking in with Daddy all the time," said Gillian, with scorn. "It's 'Yes, sir; yes, sir; yes, sir', all the time."

"That's enough, Gillian. Remember the boy must feel a bit lonely and strange. After all, your father's the only one among us he knows."

"I don't think he feels lonely, Mummy. I still think he's laughing at us, all the time; not just at Daddy, but at you too, Mummy, and Grannie, and Alistair. Even at me," she added grimly.

"I don't want you to say such things, Gillian." But Mary found it hard to make her sternness convincing; she too still had that same suspicion.

"I'm jolly well going to keep an eye on him," said Gillian. "He's not going to get making a fool of Daddy if I can help it."

"I hope you're not going to spy on him? That would be horrible."

As spying was her intention, and as she considered it in the circumstances both permissible and necessary, Gillian would not deny it.

"You know how easy it is to take Daddy in," she said. "We've got to protect him."

Her mother couldn't help laughing. "In Towellan, Gillian, your father thinks the very crabs on the shore protect him."

"Just sometimes, Mummy. This boy Curdie will spoil everything, if he isn't stopped; and I'm going to stop him."

Her mother didn't know what to say.

"What about Alistair?" she asked, at last.

"Oh, he never notices anything. He's just a child. I mean, he's all right when it comes to crabs and things like that, but he never notices people."

"All right," said her mother, capitulating. "You keep a lookout. But don't do anything unkind or unfair."

A spy, Gillian knew, thus restricted would find out nothing; therefore she gave no promises.

With the rucksack on his back containing the expedition's rations, Charlie led the way. His shorts and moccasins not being dry, he wore flannels and sandals. At first Alistair, counselled by his mother, kept close to his father, even taking his hand at times, but soon he strayed to flick bees off flowers with his forefinger, seek out grasshoppers, and pluck wild rasps. Gillian marched beside her father, while Tom Curdie walked close behind with a steadfastness that irritated Gillian, although she really couldn't have said why. Perhaps it was because his face so exasperatingly told her nothing, no matter how many unexpected glances she shot at him. Once when she put out her tongue at him he paid her no more heed than if she had been a sheep. She was angry with herself for having revealed her antagonism: spies were most successful when friendly.

The path up to the ruin twisted through tall bracken, past golden whins, over red bell-heather, and through a small pinewood that smelled of pears.

Charlie rested in the wood.

"Robert the Bruce once visited Towellan Castle," he panted. "He must have walked through this wood."

Gillian had been told that several times before. Now she preferred to gaze at Tom Curdie with clinical intentness. He was seated on a green mossy lump, staring through the lilac-coloured branches and green

94

needles towards Arran. Such earnestness could only be explained as a deliberate deception; behind it he must as usual be laughing at them. But what the purpose of that laughter could be she just couldn't make out. It was a consolation that the mossy heap on which he sat was likely full of ants.

Sure enough, when, with Alistair leaping on ahead, they continued up to the ruin now visible against the blue sky, she saw Tom clutch now at one buttock and now at the other. His face lost some of its inscrutability. He began to look like a boy whom ants were biting in embarrassing places, and who, because of her presence, couldn't get rid of them.

Alistair, with a triumphant yell and brandishing an iris leaf, disappeared into the castle.

"I hope, Daddy," said Gillian, "he's got the sense not to climb those stairs again."

"By Jove, yes!" he cried, and raced for the castle. Last year Alistair had fallen on those broken stairs and gashed his knee. Mary had warned that he be kept away from them.

Gillian stared at Tom in tight-lipped frustration. Had he been Alistair she would have looked and seen the red bites for herself. That she could not do it with this boy made his strangeness suddenly overwhelming. Yet grudgingly she admired him. Stoicism in the suffering of pain was to her one of the greatest virtues. Her own brother was a cry-baby.

Then they were hailed from the castle. In an opening in the ivied wall, about fifteen feet up, appeared her father and brother. They must have climbed the forbidden stairs. Gillian frowned.

"Come on, you two," roared her father. "We've captured the castle and put the garrison to rout."

Side-by-side they walked through the heather. Gillian was still baffled; not only could she not find words to tell him why she felt so suspicious, but she had also to take care she did not forewarn him in any way. It was a spy's predicament.

"Ants' bites," she said, "aren't poisonous."

Then she raced up the slope and over the broken wall of the castle.

As soon as she had gone he slipped amidst some high bracken, removed his shorts, and searched them for ants. He found three. He did not kill them but shook them to the ground. Then he put on his shorts again and entered the castle.

Gillian smiled but said nothing.

Within the shell of the castle the turf was short and vividly green. It would have been ideal for a picnic had it not been for much sheep dung, and one weathered human excrement in a corner. Clegs were numerous, but so they were everywhere that hot afternoon.

"We'll bivouac here," said Charlie.

Unobtrusively he dropped a flat stone on top of the faeces, and wished that it had been on the defiler's head.

"Well, sit down, mates," he said. "This is a perfect spot for a camp. Do you know what I've often thought of doing?"

"What, Pop?" asked Alistair.

"Bringing a small tent up here and spending the night. A tent wouldn't be needed; a sleeping-bag would do. Wouldn't it be grand to lie and watch the stars and listen to the night cries of birds?"

"Mummy wouldn't allow it," said Gillian.

"Would this be a good place for a tent?" asked Tom.

"Excellent," cried Charlie. "You couldn't get better. Shelter from the wind. Turf like a feather bed."

"Too many clegs," grumbled Gillian, slapping one on her wrist.

"They go at sundown."

"And then the midges come out, and they're even worse."

"Gillian," cried her father, "why so doleful?"

"I'm not doleful," she said, scratching her wrist.

"What we need is a song," he cried. "What will it be?"

Often he wished to sing when no one else did, but this time the reception of his proposal astonished him. Gillian shrieked and struggled in a frenzy of revulsion to her feet; lemonade dribbled out of her cup. Alistair too was recoiling in fear and disgust. Even Tom Curdie showed horror.

Then he realised they were not looking at him at all, but at something behind him. He turned and looked. So close to him that he could have stretched out his hand and fondled its head, sat a rabbit; but that head was so monstrous that even a St Francis would have hesitated to stroke it in pity. It was a pinky-purple swollen mass, in which the eyes, bulging hugely, were no longer organs of sight. The creature sat, apparently unaware of its traditional enemies; then it moved blindly forward and collided with Charlie who hadn't been able to scramble out of its way quickly enough. Dazed, silent, with what seemed a hideous grin of bewilderment forming on that putrescent mess, it paused again, waiting, as Charlie afterwards said, with the same heart-rending patience as Mary Stuart had waited for the axe.

He had read that these rabbits ought to be put out of their misery, and he had approved. Here was a chance to practise that stern humanitarianism. To kill a rabbit one snatched it up by the ears and struck it smartly at the back of the neck: thus the theory. But here was putrescence, which would defile the hand forever. The other method was atavistic or instinctive; in his panic he adopted it. Seizing a stone, it was the one covering the excrement, he crashed it down on the rabbit.

Gillian screamed and covered her eyes; but Alistair, usually the more tender-hearted of the two, watched in fascination.

The stone lay, with the rabbit twitching under it. Mercy demanded another blow. Charlie could not bring himself to deliver it; his hands were twitching too.

"Oh, kill it, please kill it!" screamed Gillian.

It was Tom Curdie who came forward, lifted the stone, and bending over the rabbit struck it several times with surgical coolness and accuracy. Only when it lay utterly still did he drop the bloody and messy stone. Nor did he let it drop anyhow. He placed it so that it covered as much of the dead creature as possible. In spite of his care spots of blood were on his hands; he wiped them off with grass.

They fled. Charlie rammed the things into the rucksack, and escorted Gillian past the stone. Alistair did not have to be escorted; he had to be shouted on to hurry, for more than once he turned to gaze, with marvelling druidical eyes, upon the squashed creature. Tom Curdie, picking up a cup that Charlie had missed, walked after them.

They halted in the pinewood, no longer delighting in its scented shadows, but dreading to see behind every lilac bark or lichened stone or waving fern another abomination.

"That," gasped Charlie, "was myxomatosis. God forgive them."

Gillian never would. She had stopped weeping, and her red eyes were hard.

"It was like Billy-Bobtail," she said.

Billy-Bobtail had been a toy rabbit which had shared her bed for years. Because of the fluff wearing away, its head had become pinkish and one eye had been lost. She could scarcely look at Tom Curdie, who stood with his back against a tree, waiting calmly. He did not seem at all conscience-stricken, either for killing the rabbit or just for seeing it.

Charlie comforted his daughter. "Yes, it was like Bobtail," he said. "They have forgotten that the rabbit is the friend of our infancy. We count them from railway trains when we cannot really count at all."

"Rabbits eat farmers' crops," said Alistair.

His father looked uneasily at him.

"Miss Cameron said so," insisted Alistair. She was his schoolmistress, a white-haired oracle. "She said they waste millions of pounds' worth of food every year."

"So do we all, by our gluttony," muttered his father.

Alistair ignored that foolish irrelevancy. Stooping, he picked up a stone and hurled it with force. They heard it rattle in the branches of a tree.

Charlie turned to Tom. "I would like to thank you, Tom," he said.

"No!" It was Gillian who cried that.

"But, Gillian, it was Tom who put it out of its misery. I'm sorry to say I just didn't have the heart left to do it, though it was necessary. You saw yourself how necessary it was."

"He liked doing it!" she yelled.

Her father was shocked. "What a dreadful thing to say!" he cried.

"He liked it," she repeated.

Her father felt helpless. From her he looked to the slandered boy, and then to Alistair. For an instant the three children became part of the horror; in their eyes were mysteries, remote and cruel.

"Let's get away from here," he said, with a shudder. "Let's go down to the beach."

That evening he went out fishing; in its own way it was an expedition just as ill-fated as that to the castle. Gillian refused to go, although last summer she had been keener than himself. Mary, too, declined, and in addition forbade Alistair because it would be too long after his bed-time when the boat returned. That left

Tom Curdie, who was eager, too eager, Charlie thought.

Only Alistair came down to the beach to help them push off. It was an evening of surpassing stillness and clarity; yet Charlie as he rowed out felt more and more depressed and pessimistic. It seemed to him that Tom's questions on the subject of fish and fishing were asked not out of boyish interest, but rather out of the changeling's triumph at having so soon parted the family. Such an impression was of course absurd and unjust, but it kept persisting all that evening, and was encouraged by the almost uncanny absence of fish. In spite of the wealth of bait not one fish was caught.

As they rowed ashore, pulled the boat up the beach, and made their way to the house, the moon was shining brightly, and an owl was hooting in the wood. They halted outside the back door.

"Well, it wasn't very successful," said Charlie.

"I enjoyed it, sir."

Charlie yawned. "Is it possible to enjoy fishing, without catching fish?"

"Maybe we'll be luckier next time."

"Will there be a next time?"

"I hope so, sir."

Suddenly Charlie's peevishness broke out. "You've got to give us a chance, Tom. What I mean is, you keep apart from us, you never seem to let us know what you're thinking." He had deliberately used Gillian's words. "What Gillian said today at the castle was nonsense. You didn't enjoy killing that rabbit, but did you have any pity for it? No, you kept apart even then.

And I haven't heard you laughing yet. You must let your heart thaw, Tom, if we're going to be able to help you."

In the darkness he could not see that the boy was trembling and biting his lips. If it had been daylight and he could have seen those signs of physical distress, he would not have known what caused them.

Tom knew very well, perhaps better than Forbes himself, what was meant by letting his heart thaw, because it was beginning to thaw, against his wish, threatening his whole carefully built-up system of self-sufficiency. He had, for instance, enjoyed being out in the lonely boat in the dark sea more than anything else in his life; and Forbes, whom he had intended to despise and cheat, he now found himself liking, more than liking, yearning for, so that he could scarcely bear the teacher to be out of his sight. But there was the girl Gillian, who hated him; there was Mrs Forbes, who thought that in some way he was doing harm to her children; and there was Mrs Storrocks, who had been insulted because the coachman had taken him for one of the family.

All the time, too, he had to remember that he would have to go back to Donaldson's Court, and if he went back with his heart thawed by too much love for these people, and with his independence therefore destroyed by them, he would become as lost as Peerie or Chick or his brother Alec.

The long silence discouraged Forbes. He sighed.

"Good-night," he said.

"Good-night, sir."

Charlie watched the boy walk up the moonlit garden, reach the hut, and enter; then he went into the house, removed his Wellingtons, and crept upstairs. As he opened the door of his bedroom, the owl hooted again, with peculiar intensity; so that when Mary, whom he thought was asleep, spoke from the bed in the moonlight, he was confused: it was as if her voice was a continuation of the eerie bird's.

"Do you think this is a sensible time for a boy of twelve to get to bed?"

"He's thirteen."

"Don't quibble."

He was about to start undressing when he remembered he hadn't washed his hands, which smelled of spoutfish. Tom too had gone to bed without washing.

"Did you have a good catch?" Her voice was softer; but somehow he resented the effort needed to produce that softness.

"No, we didn't. We caught nothing."

"Nothing at all?"

"Not a fin."

He thought she chuckled, but when she spoke again he knew he must have been mistaken.

"I couldn't get to sleep, Charlie, because there's something worrying me."

"Can it wait till I go and wash my hands?"

From her silence he knew the question was taken as an impertinence; perhaps he had meant it as such.

"They're stinking of bait," he said.

"I can smell them."

"I'll have to go and wash them."

"All right, go and wash them."

"I'll not be long."

In spite of that promise he lingered, washing hands and face, brushing teeth, and using the W.C. But she was still waiting when he returned. Perhaps because the moon had moved in the sky he now saw her face gleaming from the bed; it was smeared with cream to soothe sunburn.

He undressed by the window, gazing out at the moonlit wood. How happy on such a night must owls and badgers be! The moon would be shining on Goat Fell, in Arran, in the midst of the moonlit sea.

"You know fine what's worrying me," said Mary. "It's this boy Curdie."

"He's only been here one day, Mary; or one and a half, if we count yesterday."

"I don't want you to go into a huff, Charlie. If we don't get this settled, our holiday's going to be spoiled."

"Get what settled?"

"It's the way he makes up to you all the time, Charlie."

"I haven't noticed it."

"Well, the rest of us have. I understand your position, Charlie, and his too, for that matter; but I won't have our own children being made to feel out of it."

"Have they complained?"

"Not yet. Alistair hasn't noticed it yet."

"And Gillian?"

"You know how proud she is. She wouldn't complain even if her heart was breaking."

104

"So we've got to breaking hearts? You should have heard her today, accusing that boy of actually liking what he had to do to the rabbit."

"I don't want to hear any more about that. She's jealous, that's all; you should see it for yourself. She thinks — and perhaps she's not far wrong — that he's trying to steal your affection."

"Is affection like money in a bank?"

She was silent.

"Do you want him sent home?" he asked.

"No, I don't," she said quietly. "He's done nothing to deserve that, so far."

"You're sure he will, though, if not tomorrow, then the next day? Do you hope he will?"

"I think we'd all be happier if he wasn't here," she said, her voice shaking with restrained anger. "But if you think I'm praying for a chance to be able to send him home, then, Charlie, you must think a lot of your wife."

"I didn't mean it that way," he muttered. "What do you want *me* to do?"

She gave up the advantage. "I just want you to remember that Alistair and Gillian are your own children. You want this holiday to do Tom good; just make sure it doesn't harm them."

He tried to laugh. "Who did I play at Roundheads and Cavaliers with? Alistair. Who helped me to put up the swing? Alistair. Whom did I look for crabs with? Alistair. Whom did I go swimming with this morning? Gillian. Who got the extra lemonade? Gillian. If Tom

Curdie was with me this evening it was simply because no one else would go with me."

She sighed. "Oh, all right. Let's hope things will sort themselves out, if we're patient and sensible. In the meantime we'd better get some sleep."

"We're going into Dunroth tomorrow, aren't we?"

"I think so."

"I suggest we leave Tom Curdie behind."

"Why?"

"To make absolutely sure he does not monopolise my attention."

"Good-night, Charlie." She turned her face to the wall.

He stood on his bare feet, thwarted. Thus could pride so easily raise a barrier between those who loved each other dearly; and the effort to remove it exhausted love itself.

Sighing, he climbed into bed. That sigh and many others were unheeded. But at last he fell asleep, and dreamed that while fishing in a boat with the whole family beside him, all strangely still and dumb like corpses, he pulled up his line and found hooked to it the rabbit that had been killed at the castle.

CHAPTER
TEN

On the bus that took them into Dunroth there were no seats and little standing room. The conductor allowed them on out of compassion; as a result, when Mrs Storrocks loudly hinted that he was a member of a conspiracy to drive holidaymakers forever from the district, he was sadly displeased and seemed to blame Charlie, who paid the fares.

The bus itself, ill-tempered and decrepit, rattled and staggered and swayed along the sea road.

Charlie, resented because of his stoutness, had to be careful how he moved. Yet he could not bear just to stand still and pass the time staring at all the hot, peeved faces; he had to risk resentment, cramp, and crick, in order to stoop and gaze out at the scenery.

In the classroom in Glasgow, mooning out at the tramcars as they lumbered along the street, he had remembered this travelling by bus from Towellan into Dunroth as a kind of lyrical journey: joyous fellow passengers, singing wheels, enchanting scenery; that had been the purged recollection, the sustaining vision. Was this swaty, jammed, cross, bumping purgatory the honest reality? And not even Mary or Gillian could blame Tom Curdie. Of all the sufferers in the bus the boy was the most patient, the least complaining.

Remembering his despondency in the boat last night, the quarrel with Mary, and the spoiling of the visit to the castle, Charlie wondered whether after all Todd was not right and he was a fraud: if his roots were healthy, would his flowers of joy, here in Towellan, wither so soon?

At last they were spewed out in Dunroth, near the pier domed like a Turkish mosque. It was very warm, but there was a pleasant breeze off the water, which was alive with little boats. The promenade was crowded. Mrs Storrocks was paradoxically pleased; instead of grumbling that all the seats were filled, and that there was scarcely room to move, she declared it was a relief to see so many people enjoying themselves after the trees and rocks of Towellan.

Music was heard from the Castle Gardens.

"I don't know what you're going to do, Charlie," said Mary, "but we're going to listen to the 'Go-as-you-please' for a little while."

"I want to go out in a 'drive-yourself' motor-boat," said Alistair.

"Well, your daddy can take you and Tom."

"Good. Come on, Pop."

The last time Charlie had been in command of such a boat it had broken down; he had had to be towed in. It happened fairly often, it could happen to anyone, even to the chief engineer on the *Queen Mary*; but he had felt disgraced in the eyes of his son.

"Later," he muttered. "Let's go with the others first."

"Ugh, I don't like it," cried Alistair.

"I thought your father didn't like it, either," said Mary.

"I can put up with it."

"Well, remember, Charlie, we enjoy it and we don't want our enjoyment spoiled."

"Am I such a hoo-doo?" he muttered.

She laughed. "You can be, at the 'Go-as-you-please'."

As they walked through the gardens below the castle towards the music that grew louder Alistair kept on grumbling that he would rather go out in a motor-boat.

Gillian turned sharply on him. "Don't be a pest, Alistair," she said. "Daddy said he'd take you. We've just arrived, haven't we? You're a little nuisance with your harping on all the time."

Her reward was to have her brother's tongue put out at her; and from her father's expression it seemed that he would have liked to put his out too.

Mary noticed and laughed.

He paid the money which let them through the barrier to the seats. A large number of the audience hadn't considered the entertainment worth the sixpence for a seat. Dozens of them remained outside the enclosure and sat on newspapers in grassy nooks among the trees and flowers. When they departed at the end they would leave those newspapers behind. While they were there they would eat sweets and lick ice-cream: wrappings and cartons would also be left, so that the whole area would be littered. It seemed to Charlie that the garbage was symbolical of the cultural

109

rubbish that for the next hour or so would torment his ears and desecrate the sunny air. But he kept the opinion to himself this afternoon.

The first call from the platform was for competitors between the ages of five and ten. The master of ceremonies didn't have to do much coaxing. Within a minute or two a stream of volunteers, some younger than five, headed for the platform, eager to parade themselves. Charlie, disgusted by this mockery of Scottish pride and reserve, noticed how in most cases the children were abetted by their mothers.

Mary, like everybody else round him, was applauding and laughing in delight at the antics of one toddler, who couldn't have been more than three, and who went forward to the contest with pink breeks showing under her white dress, and with a pink ribbon as large as a propeller in her hair. Better, thought Charlie, if she should fly off, above the heads of these who were encouraging her to prostitute the daintiness and quaintness of her infancy, above the monkey-puzzle tree in front of the castle, and over the sea to Arran.

The performance began. First was the mite with the big ribbon. The microphone couldn't be lowered far enough so that she had to stand on a chair. With consummate showmanship she clapped her hands before she began, in a self-congratulatory fashion, and then, while the audience was convulsed with affection, she broke into shrill solemn song about a baby's dimple. Once or twice she forgot the words and gazed round blandly until she remembered again, whereupon she resumed without a flicker of embarrassment. When the audience joined in the chorus, she frowned and waggled her hands in protest; they were, it was obvious, stealing her thunder. They loved her all the more, and at the finish, when she had gently to be forced to abandon the microphone, she was rewarded with applause that might have been heard by passengers in a liner at that moment steaming down the Firth.

Next came a boy with a tartan shirt, blue jeans, sly grin, and snapping fingers. At once he burst into a shrieking, wailing, sobbing cacophony, with his arms now held out in passionate entreaty, now clasped in front of him in prayer, and now flung above his head in dramatic sorrow. But all the time his face remained cool, deliberate, crafty. At the end he, too, was clapped like mad. As he slouched off the platform, swaying his shoulders and chewing gum, he jerked his thumb upwards to someone in the crowd, perhaps his proud mother, with a flick of his head as if to indicate how easily triumph came to him.

Charlie saw, with gratitude, that Mary wasn't clapping very loudly.

"I can't be bothered with that," she remarked.

The next performer was a girl of about eight. She made her face as expressionless as a corpse's, and then, in a voice as soothing as a shovel being scraped across a stone hearth, she began to shriek about her heart being lost, and all the time waggled her backside as if, Charlie thought, she wanted to lose it, too. Here was an imitation of what she had seen often in films: all the sordid frustration of night-club cocktail-swilling adulterous society was expressed by her with shocking expertness. She ought to have been received by a profound mourning silence, broken perhaps by sighs of pity; on the contrary, hands everywhere among the flower-beds flashed like the wings of butterflies. She acknowledged them by clasping her hands above her head and ogling the whole concourse.

Mary was laughing, and clapping temperately.

"Silly wee besom," she said.

"She could do with her bottom skelped, that one," said Mrs Storrocks, and won a smile from her son-in-law.

Another diminutive crooner was offending the air; and so it went on when it was the turn of the age group ten to fifteen.

Charlie rebelled. Forgetting his huff with Gillian, he whispered to her: "How would you like to go up there and play some Scots melodies on the piano?"

She smiled but shook her head.

"Don't be daft," said Mary.

"What would be daft about it? Is there to be nothing native? Are we to be swamped by this rubbish?"

He glanced at Alistair, but saw no hope in him: Alistair had inherited musical obtuseness from himself.

"I'll go and sing a Scots song, if you like, sir."

It was Tom who offered. Charlie remembered that Miss Chisolm, the music mistress, had once remarked on the excellence of the boy's singing voice. He would, she had said with ironic giggle, have made a fine leading choir-boy in an English cathedral.

He hesitated to accept the offer. "What Scots song do you know?"

112

"'Turn ye to me', sir."

It was one of Charlie's favourites: loneliness, unhappy love, sea-sorrow. Perhaps it was too good for this audience. At the same time he remembered Mary's warning last night about keeping Tom at a discreet distance. Gillian too was looking at him strangely.

"All right, Tom," he said, recklessly. "Go and sing it, for my sake."

Politely Tom slipped out and joined the queue waiting to perform.

Mary was astonished; she hadn't been listening to the conversation. "What's he up to?" she asked.

"He's just gone to sing, that's all."

"Did you give him permission?"

"Yes."

She gave him a look then, which plainly asked if he had already forgotten all that had been said last night in their bedroom. It was an unjust look, as he indicated.

"Wait and see how he does," advised Mrs Storrocks. "One thing I'll tell you, he'll not be nervous."

She was right. None of his predecessors, not even the nightclub queen, had shown more assurance. When the microphone was lowered for him, he adjusted it a little more. Though he had never sung solo to the accompaniment of a piano, he arranged matters with the pianist without fuss. When the name of his song was announced, there was only one guffaw of derision, but it was from a mop-headed teddy-boy, who was immediately rebuked by an old woman sitting beside him. Charlie saw the incident and was elated. He flexed his fingers ready to clap like Goliath, even though Tom should break down after the first few words.

As soon as Tom began, Charlie's hands relaxed. Here, he knew, was a song and a singer that every Scottish heart must love. Without the slightest flamboyance of gesture, and yet with proper pride, Tom sang so clearly and so movingly, that even the mopheaded teddy-boy began to contemplate the brass rings on his shoes with almost aesthetic appreciation. Everywhere people's faces lit up, their mouths smiled, their hearts yearned.

"Hushed by thy moaning, lone bird of the sea,
Thy home on the rocks is a shelter to thee,
Thy home is the angry wave,
Mine but the lonely grave,
Ho ro Mhairi dhu, turn ye to me."

The applause was spontaneous and prolonged. Again the white butterflies flashed among the flower-beds; everywhere faces were like flowers of peace and happiness. Charlie wanted to shout out how he loved them all, and how he repented having misjudged them: they were not cultural degenerates, they were not mercenary pleasure-seekers, they were not litter-louts, they were human beings, lovable, mortal, and susceptible to true sorrow. While he thought thus his hands banged like carpet-beaters.

But one pair of hands did not clap; one face stayed dour: hands and face belonged to his own daughter.

114

"Why don't you clap, Gillian?" he asked, passionately. "It was beautifully sung. Are you paralysed with jealousy?"

"That's enough, Charlie," said Mary. "Surely she can clap or not clap, as she wants?"

"I didn't think any daughter of mine would be so consumed by jealousy."

"There's no jealousy in it," said Mrs Storrocks. "Maybe she's like me and thinks the song was a bit on the sad side for an occasion like this."

"You wouldn't clap, Gillian," he murmured tragically, "you wouldn't clap."

"You're being childish, Charlie," said his mother-in-law. "There are times when it seems to me that clapping's a heathenish sort of thing, not much better than rubbing noses together."

"I'm terribly disappointed in you, Gillian," he said.

She sat pale-faced and miserable, but without a tear.

When Tom came forward to rejoin them he was complimented by several people, all of them elderly.

Charlie heard with full heart. His own gratitude was simply expressed. "Thank you, Tom," he said. "That was delightful."

"Very nice, Tom," murmured Mary.

"You're a good wee singer," said Mrs Storrocks, "but you should have chosen a cheerier song."

Charlie shook his head and smiled. Tom smiled in return, but — or so Mary thought, watching as closely as Gillian the spy ever could — his smile was by no means conceited or confident or proud; nor was it a toady's smile. It seemed to her, indeed, to have hidden behind it a great deal of anxiety and unhappiness. Perhaps, then, this was the boy's true state all the time: his reserve and reticence did not, as she had thought, conceal slyness and deceit. She would have to try to be warmer towards him.

They made for the main street.

"What about the 'drive-yourself' motorboat?" demanded Alistair.

"I think we should have tea first," said his mother.

His father agreed.

Mrs Storrocks took out her purse and handed a half-crown to each of her grandchildren. "Buy what you want," she said. Then she turned to Tom. "I suppose you know how to spend money too?" And she handed him a half-crown.

From his expression Mary thought for a moment he wouldn't take it or else would take it and throw it down; but she was wrong; he took it much more politely than Alistair or Gillian had done.

She was annoyed with herself for that quite unnecessary comparison. She had scolded Charlie for it, and now it was becoming an obsession with her.

"Let's go into Woolworth's," said Alistair.

They followed him in.

CHAPTER
ELEVEN

Despite his anger and disappointment, Gillian was still devoted to her mission as her father's protectress; even more so now, because only when Tom Curdie was found out, would he become as close to her again as he had been last summer.

Accordingly, when they went into Woolworth's, which was packed with sauntering holiday-makers, it suited her when Tom at once let himself be separated from the others. She was sure this separation was deliberate on his part, as if he did not want any of them to see what he was going to buy. Likely it was sweets or chocolate which he would eat selfishly in the hut at night. Or perhaps, in the furtherance of his scheme to suck in, he intended to buy a present for her father and wanted it to be a sly surprise.

It was easy in the crowd to keep behind him, seeing but not being seen. He halted beside a counter full of small household articles. Gillian's view of him was momentarily blocked by a stout woman in a red dress, but she did not worry as it was hardly likely he would buy anything there. Then the massive red barrier moved away just in time for her to see him snatch up some small object and walk away, slipping it into his trouser pocket in the least suspicious way possible.

Shocked, fascinated, and in a dreadful way satisfied, Gillian looked round to see who else had seen. She expected a dozen customers and every attendant to be glaring and shouting at him, and at her, too, for she could not help feeling guiltily involved. But there was no one glaring, no one shouting "Thief!" The girl who attended to that particular counter was busy at its other end serving a lady who seemed hard to please, and no shopwalker was near. As Gillian walked on, her legs felt weak and her hands trembled, as if they too had just stolen. So far as she could make out in her agitation, what he had lifted was either a tin-opener or a thing for mending holes in pots. Even as presents for her mother, these were surely stupid thefts, especially as he had plenty of money to buy them.

Following him now in terrible anticipation, she saw him steal only once more: this time she was sure it was a tin of ointment. Again it seemed to her incredible that he should have wanted to steal that, unless, of course, the ant bites he had got yesterday were still painful, and he thought the ointment would ease them. She felt then even more implicated, for if she had let him get rid of the ants immediately, the bites wouldn't have been so serious. But the half-crown which her grandmother had given him would have bought both tin-opener and ointment, with change over; and he also had the money given to him by the people in the train.

To her alarm he halted at the jewellery counter and openly examined the brooches. The attendant was standing right opposite, watching him. Gillian had to restrain herself from rushing and dragging him away; if he was caught, all of them would be shamed, her father especially. But when he began to speak to the girl and she spoke back, smiling, Gillian grew calm again and walked along to him, as if the meeting was casual.

"Is this the lady?" asked the girl.

He glanced up, saw Gillian, and blushed faintly.

"No," he whispered.

Gillian smiled brightly. "What is it you're thinking of buying, Tom?" She tried to put no peculiar emphasis on that second-last word.

"A brooch."

"Is it for some girl-friend at home?" she asked.

"It's for your mother."

"Oh." Although she smiled, still more brightly, she hated him then more than she had ever done. With his hands which had so recently stolen he was coolly touching these brooches, one of which he was going to give to her mother.

"She'd like this one," she said, picking up one shaped like a butterfly.

He shook his head.

"He seems to know what he wants," said the girl.

"This one." It was in the shape of a heart, and though Gillian did not think it as pretty as the one she'd recommended, it was three shillings dearer.

"Can you afford that?" she asked.

Ignoring her, he handed it to the girl.

"Would you like me to put it in a wee box for you?" she asked.

"Thank you," he said.

When the girl had gone for the box, Gillian was tempted to whisper to him that she had seen him stealing. It irritated her almost beyond endurance to see him so calmly count out the money for the brooch.

The girl returned with the brooch in a little tartan box. Tom again thanked her and paid. Then they made for the door where they had seen the others waiting for them.

Out on the sunny thronged pavement they saw the others looking into a shop window a few yards along.

Gillian could withhold no longer.

"I saw you," she whispered. "I saw you stealing."

She had feared he would deny it with his customary impenetrable coolness, giving her no glimpse behind; but she did catch one glimpse, and it dismayed her. What she had seen was not a sneak and toady found out, but only a boy of her own age, smaller even than she, and much more perplexed and unhappy. She noticed, too, for the first time that one of his ears was slightly larger than the other.

Yet he was a thief.

"A tin-opener and a tin of ointment," she said.

He put up his hand and slowly pushed his hair back from his brow; it was a gesture of despair.

"I'll have to tell," she said, and then hurried to join her parents. "Tom's got a present for you, Mummy."

Mary glanced from her daughter to Tom; he seemed upset by having his surprise spoiled.

"Well, that's Tom's business," she said, "and mine."

"From what I saw, Gillian," said Charlie, "you seemed to spend your time wandering around, buying nothing for anybody." As he said it he knew it was unfair: no child could be more generous than Gillian in the buying of presents for friends.

"Look what I bought," cried Alistair, holding up a plastic aeroplane.

"Gillian's got sense," said Mrs Storrocks. "She knows the holiday's young yet."

"Let's go for tea," said Mary.

The presentation of the brooch was made while they were waiting for their fish and chips to be brought. Their table was by the window, out of which they had a fine view of the Firth. White-sailed yachts raced past. A large tanker steamed placidly towards the ocean. Little rowing-boats, abrupt as water-spiders, played near the beach, on which many people were sunning themselves.

What Gillian had wished, and spied for, had happened; but instead of rejoicing she was dismayed. This secret in her mind must be told and must do Tom great harm, but it did not make her clear of him, rather did it bind her to him in a way she couldn't understand or avoid; and when it was told, and he was in trouble as a consequence, even then she would not be free of him, but involved still more closely.

It had to be told. She considered telling there in the restaurant while everybody was relaxed and her parents were amiably agreeing about the fine weather; but it seemed too cold-blooded, especially as she knew he had already in his hand the box containing the brooch for her mother.

When so modestly he held out the box she felt a stab of doubt as to whether he had stolen at all; perhaps it was her spite which had made her imagine it. Thieves surely always slunk, scowled, whined, and were nasty. She began to realise that this armour, of calmness and patience, forged somehow in the dreadful slum where he had been born, must be heavy and painful to wear.

"This is for you, Mrs Forbes," he said, placing the box on the table in front of her.

His hand shook so slightly only an observer as intimate as Gillian would have noticed.

Mrs Forbes looked at it and then at him. "For me, Tom? That's very nice of you." She picked it up and opened it.

Charlie beamed.

Mary held the brooch in her hand. She was surprised by its quality; she had expected one costing a couple of shillings.

"It's lovely, Tom. It must have cost far too much, but it's really lovely. Thank you. Look at it, Mother."

Mrs Storrocks took it and admired it. She gave Tom a grim nod of approval.

"I'll treasure it always," said Mary.

Charlie asked to see it; his inspection was reverent.

"You've got good taste, Tom," he said. "Did Gillian help you to choose it? Was that what you two were conferring about?"

"No," said Gillian, with a coldness she had not meant.

Her father was saddened by that coldness. Here was the poor, despised lad from the slum buying his wife a lovely brooch, and his own daughter refused to give him a glimmer of credit.

"I hope you're remembering, Tom," said Mary, "that you'll have to take back a nice present for your own mother."

"No," he said.

There was a quality in his saying, or moaning almost, of that single word which caused even Alistair to stop flying his aeroplane over the tablecloth and look up. As for the adults, they glanced at one another; even Mrs Storrocks was silenced.

Gillian frowned.

CHAPTER
TWELVE

All that evening her mother's new brooch did not glint so brightly in the sunshine as Gillian's secret in her mind. When Alistair picked up, on the beach, a large shell, and in spite of his grannie's warning against infection held it to his ear, she had a sensation of holding something far more dangerous to hers and hearing sounds darker, more mysterious, and more baleful than any sea's. Though it sharpened her terror the presence of her victim became necessary, so that she followed him about, and sat beside him in the bus going home to Towellan.

Her persistence in keeping him company was noticed. Her father even complimented her on it; he took it to be her way of atoning for her unfriendliness and jealousy. Her mother, too, was satisfied with that easy explanation; but later, when she was washing Gillian's hair in the bathroom, she teased her about it.

"What made you and Tom become so pally all of a sudden?" she asked. "Was it because of the brooch?"

Head bent over the wash-hand basin, eyes closed, and face hidden, Gillian knew that this must be the time to tell; if she lied or evaded now, she might not be believed afterwards. Her father could be heard out on

124

the lawn with Alistair and Tom, having a last noisy game of putting.

"I saw Tom stealing today," she said.

Her mother's hands stopped in her hair.

"In Woolworth's," she added.

Her mother slowly resumed massaging. Her voice seemed to come from a distance.

"I hope you realise what you're saying, Gillian?"

"Yes, Mummy."

Mrs Forbes was silent. They could hear Charlie bellowing congratulations to Alistair who had done a hole in one. They could picture Alistair's glee and pride; and they could picture Tom Curdie standing by, smiling.

"This is a very serious accusation, Gillian. It's not a joke."

"I know, Mummy."

"He didn't steal the brooch, did he?"

"No, he bought that. But he stole the other things."

"What other things?"

"A tin-opener, I think, and a tin of ointment."

"A tin-opener and a tin of ointment!"

"Yes. It sounds silly, doesn't it? He could easily have bought them, if he wanted them; but what does he want them for? Yesterday some ants bit him, but ant bites don't last."

The warm water was now streaming through Gillian's hair; and through her mind, even more deliciously, flowed forgiveness.

"I wish he hadn't done it," she said.

Her tone made her mother suspicious. "So do I, Gillian. Were you the only one who saw him? You must have been, otherwise he'd have been caught."

"I was spying."

"I thought I told you not to."

"I'm sorry. I wish I hadn't. I'll never do it again, never."

"Now that it's served its purpose?"

"You don't think I'm just making this up, do you, Mummy?"

"I wouldn't like to think that, Gillian. But why haven't you spoken about it before this?"

"You don't believe me!" wailed Gillian. "You think I'm trying to get him into trouble." She began to sob.

"I asked you why you've kept quiet until now."

"I don't know. I didn't want to tell, but I had to."

"Why had you?"

Gillian looked at her mother in astonishment.

"But stealing's awful, Mummy!"

"Some people might say so is spying. Have you said anything to Tom?"

Gillian spoke now through sobs. "Yes, just outside Woolworth's."

"And what did he say?"

"He said no, but I could see he was frightened. I felt sorry for him. That was why I didn't want to tell you or Daddy."

"Gillian, look at me. I've got to be sure, very, very sure. Now is this the truth? Did you see him stealing?"

"Yes, Mummy."

"Your father thinks you've got a spite against the boy, and are jealous of him."

"But, Mummy, he wouldn't think I was making this up just to get Tom into trouble!"

"I hope he wouldn't, Gillian."

"But Daddy knows I tell the truth."

"He should, for you always have. But it seems to be different now; this boy has bewitched us all."

"Maybe he couldn't help it, Mummy. Some people are like that, aren't they?"

"So they say. But if Tom stole he could help it all right."

"You said if. You don't really believe me, Mummy."

"Yes, I do. You see, he *is* a thief." Mary realised she ought not to have said that, but it was too late now. "He's on probation for stealing," she added irritably. "That's partly why your father brought him here. He thought there was good in him, as I suppose there is. But bringing him here certainly hasn't brought it out. He's caused nothing but trouble since he came. And we're just three days here. It seems like a month."

"Maybe we shouldn't tell Daddy."

Mary was again suspicious. "Why not?"

"It'll upset him."

"It'll certainly do that."

"Then why should we? I wanted to help Daddy, not upset him."

"If Tom's a thief, that's not your fault. No, he'll have to be told, and I'm afraid Tom will have to be sent home."

"But, Mummy, wouldn't it be better to let him stay and try to teach him that stealing's wrong?"

Was that, Mary wondered, Sunday-school righteousness, or mawkish deceit?

"I think Tom knows very well stealing's wrong," she said. "Whatever he is, he's no fool. But I'll have to talk it over with your father. In the meantime say nothing to your grandmother."

Supper for Charlie was a jolly meal that evening. While putting he, Alistair, and Tom had established a comradeship; now at the table he made sure it continued. Gillian, who wore a towel like a turban round her head, was the subject of some of his witticisms, at which his own daughter was by far the heartiest. He named her the Queen of Sheba, and kept referring to her by it. He did not notice Mary's frown of warning, but he did notice that she wasn't wearing her new brooch. When he asked her why she said quietly she'd to take it off while washing Gillian's hair lest it should scratch her face. He accepted the excuse but insisted that it now be pinned on again. Indeed, he himself rose to go and fetch it; whereupon, more harshly than she meant, Mary told him to sit where he was: when she wanted to wear the brooch, she would wear it. He was deflated, and his winks at the two boys, and at Gillian, too, could not blow up his merriment again.

When the children were in bed Mary proposed that they should go for a short stroll along the shore. Charlie was pleased but demurred for her sake: he thought that walking about Dunroth that day must have tired her out. So it had, she replied, leaving him still pleased but also puzzled and a little apprehensive.

"I see," he murmured shyly, as they walked down the path, "you're still not wearing your brooch."

"You'll be expecting me to sleep with it on."

"Mary, you must forgive me if I seem to be making a great deal of it. You see, really, I regard it as the first victory, in the battle of Tom Curdie, I mean."

"You exaggerate everything, Charlie."

"Not this, Mary, not this."

It was a fine still night. A late motor-boat, full of singing holiday-makers, headed for Rothesay; its ripples in the smooth water had in them all the colours of the sky, pink, gold, blue, white, and green.

There were also midges. Mary already was waving her handkerchief and scratching. Charlie, whom they always seemed to find sourer, was not molested so much. He plucked a frond of bracken and fanned around her head with it.

She told him not to be a damned fool. He dropped the bracken.

"Perhaps we should go back?" he suggested.

"I knew there would be midges when I asked you to come out. I thought you'd have guessed there was something I've got to tell you. I've considered it and considered it until my head's dizzy. So I'm passing it on to you, Charlie. It's really your concern, or your battle as you've just called it."

He waited, with little nervous snorts.

"And for God's sake, Charlie, let's talk about it sensibly."

Still he waited, snorting.

"It's about Tom. Gillian saw him shop-lifting in Woolworth's today. So there's been no victory, Charlie. He's still a thief, and considering that he's our guest a particularly shameless one, too."

"Gillian saw him?"

"Yes. I know what you're going to say —"

"Please let me say it, Mary. Let me express my own thoughts. I'm quite capable of doing so. I think that what you really meant to say was 'Gillian says she saw Tom stealing'. There's a difference."

"I'm going to believe my own child."

"Wait a minute, Mary. You said we were to discuss this sensibly; that means surely without passion or bias. Now then. You and I and Alistair and your mother were in Woolworth's today. There were besides dozens of other people; not to mention those whose duty it is to watch out for thieving. Not one of all these saw him steal. Only Gillian. It is a curious coincidence that she too was the only one, among those two or three hundred in the Castle Gardens, who would not clap when he sang."

Mary made an effort to say nothing about his pomposity and conceit, though these had infuriated her. "It comes down to this, Charlie," she said. "Either our daughter's a nasty spiteful liar, or Tom Curdie's a thief. I think it should be taken into account that he's already been convicted of stealing."

"But that's not fair, Mary," he bleated.

130

"It's fair to Gillian."

"And that's all that matters?"

"To me? Yes."

"But couldn't it be, Mary, she's not aware of the seriousness of such an accusation?"

"She's not a fool. She knows very well how serious it is. She was crying when she told me."

"You see! Where affection's concerned children can be unscrupulous; they need it, as a bird needs air, or a fish needs water, and so they'll do anything for it; yes, they'll even lie, though in the circumstances I wouldn't call it lying."

"Curdie seems able to do without it well enough. Did you hear him when I told him to remember to take a present home to his mother? Affection? He doesn't need it, he doesn't want it, and he's not got it to give; in fact, he's more likely to take it away."

"You're making him out to be a veritable little monster, Mary; worse even than my changeling."

"He's what he is, Charlie; he's not what you think him to be."

"Evidently, though, he's what you think him to be."

"He'll have to be sent home."

"Back to the environment which has made such a monster out of him?"

"He'd have to go back in any case. You weren't proposing to adopt him for good?"

"Yes, Mary, he'd have to go back; but not under these circumstances, branded and damned."

"Are you sure you're thinking of him, Charlie? Isn't it really yourself you're worried about? Are you afraid they'll laugh at you at school when they hear you'd to send him back so soon for stealing?"

"Do you think I care for their miserable laughter? And who would be so kind as to inform them?"

"He's capable of it himself."

"Mary, if he goes, I go, too."

She gasped, and then laughed. "I hope you know what you're saying, Charlie?"

"Yes, I know. It's no laughing matter, Mary."

"Isn't it? Am I not supposed to laugh when you threaten to leave me, and the children, for the sake of your pet delinquent from the slums?"

"My pet delinquent!" he wailed. "Have mercy, Mary. If I can't have it from you, from whom am I to have it?"

"Charlie, there's no need for this desperation. You trusted him; he's let you down. It's a pity. But it's nothing to be desperate about. It's happened hundreds of times before, and it'll happen hundreds of times again. Surely you've lived long enough to know that trust isn't unbreakable."

"What was it she said he stole?"

"What difference does that make?"

"I want to know, Mary. I've got a right to know."

"A tin-opener and a tin of ointment."

"But what in Christ's name would he want those for?" he wailed.

"Don't use that language to me, Charlie."

"You called me a damned fool, Mary."

"I don't know what he wanted them for," she cried. "I don't know what goes on in his mind, and neither do you. I wish I had never set eyes on him. I'm going back to the house, Charlie. It's getting chilly."

She turned and walked back. "Are you coming?" she called.

"No, not yet. I want to think about this."

"All right. Don't stay out too long."

He stood listening, groaning, and hoping, pathetically, that she would come running back, to assure him it had all been a mistake, Tom had not stolen, Gillian had not lied, everybody was friendly, and the holiday from now on was going to be as happy and fruitful as he had dreamed. But she did not come back. He heard her walk up the gravel path to the house; he saw the door open and shut again. She was gone.

Standing in the road, he pressed his hands against his head tightly, and in that attitude, like some kind of prisoner of war, he stumbled down onto the beach where, crouching among the boulders, he began to moan and sigh.

The sea itself made many noises, tranquil and threatening no one; yet it seemed to him they were merely repeating, many times, with subtle insistent variations Todd's word: "Humbug".

Then, as he listened, those noises of the sea were no longer tranquil and neutral: they combined into a hostile indictment of him: as a man, as a husband, as a father, as a teacher, they roared, he had failed. Nor would they allow him any of his old resources or subterfuges. They reminded him that the war which had restored so many manhoods had not restored his. They brought up a picture of him sitting in the

133

staffroom listening to the younger men talk of their war exploits, in Burma, or Africa or Europe or even in some English pub uproarious with khaki'd beer-drinkers. He, reserved through age, had spent a few months on evacuation duty in a Perthshire village, and then two or three foolish years in the Home Guard. His contemporaries, like Todd, were protected by their promotion from any feeling of inferiority at having been left out of the colossal mêlée. He had no such protection; especially to his own small son in search of heroism. He was defenceless.

As he gazed over the sea he saw that the moon at last was glittering upon it, most beautifully; but the effect upon him was to drive him from his last refuge. He could no longer deny that his finding consolation in the loveliness of nature, and in his championing of the meek and oppressed against such as Todd, had been insincere. The sight of the Sleeping Warrior in the sunset sky had certainly never compensated for his lack of professional success; and his Samaritan succouring of Tom Curdie had been motivated by an intricacy of selfish hopes.

And seeing himself clearly, unobscured by self-pity, he also saw what Mary must have seen for years. It was no wonder her tolerance had given way tonight. She, who had been forced to adjust herself to the harsh ways of the world, had had to suffer his pretences to be superior to those ways, when the truth was, seen daily by her, that he was incapable even of intelligent compromise.

134

For over an hour he sat among the rocks. During that time a young couple passed on the road, linked together. They stopped to kiss. He felt a great unrevengeful pity for them, so that he wanted to cry out a warning, but he did not know what it was he should warn them against.

The light was still on in the living-room as he trudged up the path. So Mary had not gone to bed; she had waited up to see if he had come to a sensible decision; well, if to agree to send Tom home tomorrow was sensible, he had. There would be no investigation, no prolonging of the crisis. Silence and acquiescence must be his part now, until he felt sure enough of his new self to begin to have trust in it; in the meantime he would depend on Mary's advice and judgment.

As a result he was appalled by the look she cast at him as he slunk discreetly in; resentment and hatred were surely in it, turning her face almost unrecognisable. He expected her to scream at him, so that the actual quietness of her voice was all the more terrifying.

"All right," she said. "You've won."

"Won, Mary? I never felt less like a victor in my life."

"You've won."

He sat down by the fire beside her, shivering. A fragment of seaweed clung to the bottom of his trousers. He was too stiff and dispirited to pick it off.

"I'm afraid I don't understand, Mary. I'm sorry for what I said, above all, for saying I was going to leave you. God knows where I could go to."

"While you were out," she said, speaking in short gasps, as if the words were burning her mouth, "Gillian came down here, out of her bed."

He shook his head. "Poor Gillian!"

"If you dare to pity her, Charlie, as sure as God I'll strike you."

He was astounded and utterly lost.

"She came down here to take back what she'd said about Curdie."

He was so dazed with astonishment and terror at her attitude that he couldn't understand.

"She admitted she had made it up, out of spite. You were right. You judged her character perfectly. She's a nasty spiteful little liar. And Curdie's innocent, this time. So you'll be satisfied."

"Satisfied?" He almost wept the word.

"Yes, satisfied. You don't have to feel sorry for yourself any more. This is another victory, Charlie. You were right."

He wanted to cry out that he was sorry for her and Gillian, but he did not dare.

"Do you think she did it for my sake?" he asked humbly.

"Still thinking of yourself, Charlie?"

"No." He couldn't repress a long sore sigh, which was not free of self-pity. "I'm thinking of Gillian. She's a warm-hearted honest child."

"Don't start praising her now."

"I just meant she might be trying to save me from disappointment."

It was evident that Mary suspected this new tone of his, this meekness, was some kind of new strategy; self-pity, she knew, was versatile.

"That occurred to me," she said.

"Did you put it to her?"

"She'd still be a liar."

"Don't be embittered, Mary. We'll send him home tomorrow, and then we'll be able to forget the whole unhappy business."

"Why should we send him home?"

So even his unconditional surrender was to be spurned. "I thought that was what you wanted, Mary."

"I don't like having him here, you know that; but I wouldn't send him home without a good reason. If Gillian lies about him out of spite and jealousy, is that a good reason?"

"It's obvious his presence here isn't doing her any good; or any of us, for that matter."

"I won't deny that, Charlie; but if you send him home because of this, it's your responsibility, not mine."

"I respect your judgment, Mary. If you don't think I should, then of course I won't."

"There's another thing, Charlie: leave Gillian alone."

"I would never dream of punishing her."

"And I would never dream of letting you. She's been punished enough. I meant don't start pestering her to get at what you would call the truth. You're not as clever as you think, Charlie; you'd just make things a hundred times worse. She's upstairs at this minute breaking her heart — in our bed, Charlie. I told her to go there. You can sleep with Alistair. Good-night."

She was gone before he could ask if this sleeping apart was for this night only, or for the rest of the holiday. Was this the punishment she had decided on for him?

After shivering by the low fire in the silent house for another hour, suffering over again the revelations at the seashore, and becoming more and more doubtful as to what he should do, he began to give way to the feeling that he was in the grip of inimical non-human forces, whose instrument was indeed Tom Curdie.

CHAPTER
THIRTEEN

Tom had stolen the tin-opener and the ointment to convince himself he was Chick and Peerie's friend, and Alec's brother, and that his home was in Donaldson's Court, to which he must return. It was to destroy the delusion growing in his mind that Mr and Mrs Forbes were his parents, Alistair his brother and Gillian his sister, and that his home was their house in the avenue of gardens. Necessary to that delusion was another, that there was no such place as Donaldson's Court, and no such persons as Alec, Molly, his mother, Shoogle, Chick and Peerie. Everywhere in Towellan, in the garden among the rose-bushes, in the hut at night listening to the owl, on the lawn putting, even in the ruined castle with the sick rabbit, he was becoming convinced that this was the way of life he had always known and always would know; that at the end of the holiday he would return with the rest of the family, and would for the rest of his life be involved in their affairs as he was now; and that he would always have a bed to himself with clean sheets, and plenty of good food served on a table with a white cloth.

Then on the platform while he was waiting to sing those delusions had been ended. Mr Forbes and Alistair had waved at him; he had not waved back, but the man presenting the show had said: "There's your father and brother wishing you luck, but your sister doesn't look too pleased. Just you show her what you can do."

So when in Woolworth's he had picked up the tin-opener and the ointment, it had been as an acceptance of reality. The buying of the brooch for Mrs Forbes had been for the same purpose.

Gillian's seeing of him had at first dismayed him until he realised that if he went on staying with them as before the delusion would grow again. So all that evening he was resigned to her telling her parents and to their challenging him. He would at once confess but give no reason, and they would send him away. He would arrive back in the Court in time to prevent the others from coming. What the effect on him of this short stay here would be, he would find out afterwards.

But the evening passed, and though at supper-time Mrs Forbes did not wear the brooch and was angry with her husband for teasing her about it, Tom couldn't be sure that Gillian had told them. Gillian herself, wearing the turban, two or three times looked at him not only with the usual dislike but also with sadness. He had gone to bed, not knowing what had happened.

Next morning, deeper in his shell than ever, he thought that Gillian for some reason had told her father but not her mother. Mrs Forbes wore the brooch and was pleasant to him, though she was sharp-tempered with everybody else, even with Alistair. Mr Forbes, on the other hand, avoided him and went off rowing all morning with Alistair. Mrs Storrocks couldn't have been told either, because as she sat in her deck-chair on the lawn she called him from his putting to go and fetch her handbag, which she had left lying on the sofa in the sitting-room. When he went for it he thought it wiser to ask Mrs Forbes's permission to go into the sitting-room. "Why not?" she asked, with a smile, as if there could be no question in her mind as to whether or not he was to be trusted.

Gillian, like her father, avoided him; soon after breakfast she went off by herself to climb the hill behind the house.

And thus it continued till Friday, the day when he was to go into Dunroth to sing in the Final of the "Go-as-you-please" competition, and Alec, Chick, and Peerie were to arrive by steamer.

The change took place at the dinner-table.

"I suppose," said Mrs Storrocks, "though there's been less talk about it than I'd have thought, that we're all going into Dunroth this afternoon to hear Tom sing in the Final."

"Good!" cried Alistair. "*This* time we'll go out in a 'drive-your-self' motor-boat."

"I don't see why not, Mother," said Mrs Forbes. "It's a lovely afternoon."

"Can I stay at home?" asked Gillian.

Her father spoke in a quiet, sad voice. "We are all going to stay at home, Tom included."

Tom knew it was to make sure he didn't steal again.

"What's this?" cried Mrs Storrocks. "He's not to be allowed?"

"I would rather not discuss it, Mrs Storrocks," said Mr Forbes, in that same voice. He looked at his wife as if for support, but she did not seem willing to give it.

"If you think, Charles," cried Mrs Storrocks, "you can adopt such a high-handed and mysterious manner with me, you're far mistaken. Can you tell me what this is about, Mary?"

Mrs Forbes smiled, but it seemed to Tom she was near to weeping. "Don't bring me into it, Mother. I don't want to go. I had enough of it on Tuesday."

"I understood, Mary, you thoroughly enjoyed yourself on Tuesday. So it's only me and the two laddies who want to go? Very well, we'll go, and the rest of you can stay at home."

"Mrs Storrocks," said Mr Forbes, "you evidently do not understand. You may of course go to Dunroth, or any place you wish."

"There's one place in particular you're thinking of, Charles," she cried.

Tom knew the place she meant. No one smiled.

Mr Forbes shook his head. "No, no. I just want to make it clear that Tom and Alistair are not to be allowed to go into Dunroth today."

"But what for, Pop?" cried Alistair. "I'll pay my own fare."

"Fares have nothing to do with it, son."

"What has to do with it?" asked Mrs Storrocks. "You've been acting rather oddly this last day or two, Charles, like a man that's waiting to be hanged." She smiled and got Alistair to join her; no one else would.

"I don't think we should discuss this any more in front of the children," said Mrs Forbes.

"It concerns the children, Mary," said her mother, who then addressed Tom: "Do you want to go?"

He nodded: not only was he going, but he was not coming back.

"Yes, I should say so," said Mrs Storrocks. "Your attitude, Charles, quite absolutely baffles me. On Tuesday you were as proud as a dog with two heads. If he'd been one of your own you couldn't have been prouder. Look at the fuss you made because Gillian wouldn't clap. And, now, if you please, he's not to be allowed to go!"

Suddenly he crashed his fist down on the table, making dishes and cutlery rattle.

"I'm trying to do what's for the best," he cried, like a child that was trying not to weep.

Mrs Storrocks rose. "Do you think I'm going to stay here and be threatened by fists?" she said. "There's been many a hint I've not heeded, but I think it's clear enough now that I'm not welcome."

Mrs Forbes shut her eyes. "Sit down, Mother," she sighed. "Of course you're welcome."

"I wasn't referring to you, Mary. I can't be dictated to as to where I'll go or not go."

"I didn't dictate to you, Mrs Storrocks," said Mr Forbes wearily. "If I gave that impression I beg your pardon. I'm just trying to keep things going as smoothly as possible."

She laughed. "You've chosen a funny way of doing it, Charles." And she walked out.

He made to rise and try to persuade her not to go, but his wife told him sharply to sit down. When he did so he covered his face with his hands.

"What's wrong?" demanded Alistair. "Have I to go to Dunroth with Grannie?"

"You hold your tongue," cried his mother. "Tom, this concerns you most. If you want to go to Dunroth this afternoon, you may."

"What about me?" asked Alistair.

"I told you to hold your tongue."

Mr Forbes took his hands away from his face; he looked desperate, as if he didn't know what to say or even to think. "But, Mary," he wailed, "surely you understand —"

"No, I don't," she yelled.

His face was swept by anger. "I've stood as much as I can. All week I've been humiliated."

"Who's been humiliating you? Nobody that I've seen."

"Every pebble on the beach, every blade of grass on the hill," he shouted. "I've abased myself. I've crawled on my knees. And what's been my reward? Humiliation."

"Gillian, Alistair, Tom," said Mrs Forbes, "leave the room."

"But I've not finished my milk," grumbled Alistair.

"Then leave the bloody thing," roared his father. "Go on, get out. Not you, Gillian. I want you to stay. And you, too, Tom."

Alistair went out crying.

Mrs Forbes was on her feet. She had a knife in her hand as if, thought Tom, she was minded to throw it at her husband. Her face was so full of hate she seemed to him vividly like Gillian.

"You gave me your promise, Charlie," she said.

"Mary, can't you see, this thing's round my neck, choking me? Your mother was right, I have been going about like a man about to be hanged. There's a fog of doubt and suspicion and distrust in this house. It must be dispelled, once and for all." He turned towards Gillian, with what he tried to make a conciliatory smile. "Gillian my dear, please listen to me."

She began to scream: "No, no, no. I'm not going to say anything. Mummy, please!" And she ran to her mother, who embraced her.

"Gillian, Gillian," wailed her father, "don't think I don't love you."

In her mother's arms she sobbed bitterly.

Mr and Mrs Forbes looked at each other like strangers. It seemed to Tom that he knew them better then than they knew themselves.

Suddenly Gillian struggled out of her mother's embrace and rushed from the room.

Mr Forbes turned to Tom. "So you want to go and sing?" he asked harshly.

"Yes, sir."

"Are you so keen on winning the money?"

"I'd like to try, sir."

Forbes sneered and quoted: " 'Thy home is the angry wave, Mine but the lonely grave'. You may go and sing. My rudder is broken."

Tom looked at Mrs Forbes. He was astonished by the loathing in her eyes; but she nodded, and he immediately left the room.

As he went through the hall to the front door he caught sight of Forbes's old raincoat hanging on a peg. It was soiled, with green paint on its seat. He had a longing to touch it, but that shy gesture could not satisfy the sudden surge of love in him, so that he crushed his face into the coat, smelling not only paint but the sea.

As he stood thus he heard a noise and thought it might be Gillian again spying on him; but when he looked round there was no one. It must have been the grandfather clock. Mr Forbes often said "Pardon" on its behalf: it was one of the family's jokes. Tom was reminded of Shoogle, who also said "Pardon"; but this massive mahogany clock, inlaid with brass, was taller and in every way handsomer and more durable than the small, belching, drunken cripple.

Then Tom found himself not hurrying through the garden to the hut, but knocking at the dining-room door. He would confess not only to the thefts in Woolworth's but also to the others at school; and he would tell them he was going away that afternoon for good.

Mr Forbes opened the door, just enough to show his face; tear-stained, bewildered, and woebegone, it might have struck a stranger as comical. Inside the room was the sound of Mrs Forbes weeping.

"What is it?" muttered Mr Forbes. "What d'you want?"

146

What Tom had come to say, he found he could not; that weeping within the room demoralised him; or rather it drove him back to his old resources.

"I was wondering, sir," he said politely, "if I could have a loan of the bike to go to Dunroth."

"The bike?" repeated Forbes.

"Yes, sir. It would save the bus fare."

There was a rush inside the room. Forbes was pushed aside and his wife's face was seen, tearful, enraged, ugly.

"No, you can't have the bicycle," she screamed. "You knew Gillian was going to use it; that's why you want it."

Not only had he not known that, but he thought Mrs Forbes hadn't known it either.

"I didn't know, Mrs Forbes," he murmured.

"Yes, you did. You can't have it. Do you hear, you can't have it!"

Then she rushed back into the room.

Forbes was left glaring miserably out at him.

"Changeling," he muttered. "Changeling."

It was a word Tom did not know. Then the door was closed.

CHAPTER
FOURTEEN

It was only twenty past two when the bus took him into Dunroth. After making sure that the steamer was due at five past three he went for a walk up through the gardens, passing the Union Jack shaped with rockery plants, and the Crown with fairy-lights round it. People dressed for sunshine were putting on the green, or picnicking in grassy corners; a long row of them sat on the benches along the castle terrace, where there were many flowers as bright as the women's dresses, bees, a flag-pole without a flag, and a monkey-puzzle tree without monkeys. He walked slowly, needing the people's company in a way he had not done before. Hitherto he had moved among them like a spy among un-acknowledged enemies; now he was more than ever on the lookout, but this time it was for companionship and especially for assurance that he was like them all, able and permitted to look at what was lovely and laugh at what was funny.

As he stared down from the high terrace to the blue Firth, two or three times, hearing a man's laughter, he turned with a stound at his heart, expecting to find Mr Forbes beside him; for it was Mr Forbes who had compared the flowers to the women's dresses, and who had looked in the tree for the puzzled monkeys.

From there steamers could be seen leaving the pier four or five miles across the water. Seeing what he took to be the one due in at five-past three with Alec, Chick, and Peerie on board, he was about to wander down towards the sea-front when he noticed a woman coming out of the big castle-like building with books under her arm. Going over, he saw a notice saying it was a library and reading-room. Although he knew that children not accompanied by adults were seldom allowed into libraries, he entered. Often in Glasgow he had been privileged, despite his clothes; he had sat for hours, as in a sanctuary, studying encyclopaedias, atlases, and history books; often he had done his school exercises there.

Inside was an empty hall with stairs. On the top was a door with the name "Reading-Room" on it. There was another, inscribed "Toilet", with the "i" almost erased. He saw the joke, in this town of landladies.

The reading-room was really a sunken corner of the library which was reached by a short flight of steps. There was no door, so that Tom could see the librarian behind the counter. She in her turn could see him. Once or twice she seemed about to come and find out what he was doing there, but changed her mind, no doubt because of his quiet purposefulness. He it was who went to her.

"Could I have a look at a dictionary, please?" he asked.

"And what do you want a dictionary for?" But she was amused rather than displeased.

"To look up a word."

"What word?"

"Changeling. Is there such a word?"

"Yes, there is." She was now surprised.

"I'm not sure what it means."

"No, it's not a very common word. Is it for a competition?"

"No."

"Are you on holiday here?"

"Yes."

She went into a room behind the counter and returned with a large dictionary, which she set down in front of him.

"Do you know how to use it?"

"Yes, thanks."

Quickly he turned over the pages. He ran his finger down the columns till at last it stopped at the word he wanted. "Changeling: a creature, in animal or human form, supposed to be left by the fairies or 'other folk' in place of one they had stolen; often applied to a dwarfish, ill-favoured person or animal, spreading an evil influence."

He read it several times, until he could have repeated it by heart, seeing more and more clearly why Mr Forbes had applied it to him, and why Mrs Forbes had looked at him with such loathing. When the librarian smiled at him, he hardly knew how to smile back. A sense of strangeness possessed and frightened him; his finger on the dictionary did not look like a finger at all.

"Well, did you find it?" asked the librarian.

"Yes, thanks," he whispered.

"It's a funny word to be looking up."

"Yes. I think it was a kind of joke."

All the way down to the pier he felt that strangeness. The people whose company he had enjoyed were now remoter than ever; the assurance of kinship had been taken away. He could not bear to think about the Forbes family; whenever his thoughts strayed near them they recoiled, as if from an area of pain, terror, and shame.

As the steamer edged in to the pier he could not at first make out his friends, so many hands were waving. Then he heard a screech shriller than any seagull's; it was made by Chick whom he now saw, wearing a skipped cap of four colours. Beside him stood Peerie with a similiar cap. There was no sign of Alec.

People laughed as Chick and Peerie came staggering down the gangway, laden with tent, pans, blankets, and rucksacks. Both wore tight blue jeans. Peerie's were genuinely American, with galloping cowboys sewn on; his shirt too was gaudier than Chick's tartan. Each had his hair rumped close.

They greeted him with typical grimaces, winks, yelps, and pokes in the belly. It was Peerie, the soft-hearted, who noticed Tom did not respond.

"Are you feeling sick, Tom?" he asked. "You look sick."

Chick was already leering round at the girls in their brief shorts and sleeveless blouses. "Peerie was nearly sick on the boat," he said, "and it was as calm as a pail o' piss." He winked at his joke, spat, and flicked at a fag-end behind his ear.

Peerie grinned. "Chick was talking aboot things that would make onybody sick," he said. "Alec couldnae come, Tom."

"Boils," said Chick, "all over his mug."

"You said, Tom, we'd to come even if Alec couldnae manage." Peerie smiled as he spoke, but could not coax a smile out of his leader.

Chick thrust his face near theirs. "See that one?" he whispered, and winked towards a girl of about sixteen, proud of her breasts in their white silken jumper, and of her long tanned legs naked to the thighs. "I could go for that."

Peerie stared at Tom and grinned in shame. "He's always talking about tarts noo."

"I'm growing up," said Chick, grabbing himself lewdly. "Whit aboot this tart you're staying wi, Tom? Whit's she like? Skinny? Nae tits yet?"

"That's whit I mean, Tom," whispered Peerie.

Suddenly Tom seized Chick by the front of his shirt. He could not speak.

Chick glanced at Peerie in amiable surprise. Peerie also couldn't understand this violence on the part of his gentle leader.

"There's folk watching," he warned.

"You'll tear aff the buttons," said Chick, smiling.

"Don't speak aboot them," whispered Tom.

"Who's them?" asked Chick. He had already forgotten his remarks about Gillian; his eyes were again roving.

Tom let go. "The people I'm staying with," he said.

Chick smoothed his shirt. "O.K."

"You're an awfu' toff, Tom," said Peerie, eagerly. "When we saw you on the pier Chick said it wasnae you, you were such a toff."

Tom remembered his singing. He must try to win, for the money was needed. When he walked away, they staggered after him with their loads.

"I'm bigger than you, Tom," remarked Chick.

Peerie was always the peacemaker. "There'll be room in the tent for you, Tom, seeing Alec's no here."

Tom didn't answer.

Peerie was anxious. "My grannie said she wouldnae let me come if you werenae to be staying in the tent wi us."

"His grannie doesnae trust me," chuckled Chick.

They crossed the street towards the gardens. A girl was singing; amplified, her voice yearned for her lover to come back to her.

Chick was enchanted. "Whit smashin' singing. She'll hae a face like a donkey's bum, but she can sing."

"Where are we going, Tom?" asked Peerie.

"It's a competition. I'm in the Final."

They were delighted.

"Whit's the prize?" asked Chick.

"Three pounds."

"Whit are you going to sing, Tom? Make it the 'Unchained Melody'. Like this." He sang a piece: " 'Oh, my love, my darling, I have hungered for your touch'."

Leaving them, Tom hurried round behind the stage. His fellow-finalists were already on it. The master of ceremonies waved him up.

"I thought you'd gone away home," he said. "Are you singing the same as on Tuesday?"

Tom nodded.

"That's right. Are your folks here again?"

That last question was accompanied by a glance over the audience for the proud parents. He was flabbergasted therefore when Tom suddenly turned, jumped off the stage, and disappeared.

Tom rejoined his friends. Paying no heed to their astonished questions, he hurried down to the beach.

"Did you see a detective?" gasped Peerie.

"There were some guys saying you would win," said Chick.

"If you had won that three pounds," said Peerie, sadly, "we might no hae needed to steal."

Chick glanced about with predatory eyes. He saw a woman lying on her back on the grass, asleep, her mouth open, her belly rising and falling. Her bag lay beside her; so did her man, but he was a wee bald stupid man who could be robbed easily.

"Just let me get started," he said. "I'm going to like this place: plenty of tarts and money."

"My grannie said I wasnae to steal," persisted Peerie.

"Your grannie's a daft auld bitch," said Chick. "Do you know whit she did, Tom? She made us promise no to steal."

"On the Bible," added Peerie.

"Aye, but it had nae batters," said Chick. "You can swear onything by a Bible that's got nae batters."

"My grannie's deeing."

"She's been deeing for years."

"She likes you, Tom," said Peerie, "and you said you liked her."

That was true: Grannie Whitehouse had been the only person in Donaldson's Court whom he'd respected; though very poor and old, she had never given in. But it was different now.

"Sure you said you liked her, Tom?"

"I liked her, Peerie."

"I'm going to bring her rock," said Peerie, in a trembling voice. "Dunroth rock, wi the name right through it."

They were by this time seated in a nook among rocks on the shore. Chick was watching three plump women in bathing costumes; they were throwing a beach ball at one another. One's buttocks kept oozing out so that she had to keep pushing them back in.

"Where are we going to put up the tent, Tom?" asked Peerie.

"There's a big hoose on the cliff," said Tom. "It's empty. It's like a castle. Maybe it was burnt doon years ago. But there's a bit of the roof still on. Maybe it would be better than the tent."

Chick had stiffened. "Whit aboot ghosts?"

They weren't surprised by this question: Chick, they knew, was often haunted; he didn't like darkness or derelict houses; he didn't like old women.

"We've told you a thousand times, Chick," said Peerie, "that there are nae ghosts nooadays."

"Whit about the folk that were burnt to daith in the fire?"

155

"If there was onybody burnt, Chick, then they're deid."

"I could see them in the middle of the night." He seemed to see them then, in the bright sunshine, on the crowded beach. "They'd hae hair like fire."

Peerie giggled in nervous sympathy. He knew that if in the dark broken house Chick saw those ghosts with hair like fire he might see them, too.

Chick's white face, which no sun would ever tan, and his weird eyes, became to Tom strangely familiar. In the library, reading the dictionary, he had tried to imagine what a changeling would look like; here now, seated beside him, was such a creature.

In revulsion he leapt to his feet and ran down the beach towards the water.

Peerie gazed after him, in dismay. "Whit's the matter wi Tom?" he asked. "He'll no talk to us. He's different."

Chick did not hear. A woman had gone behind a rock to dress. He had not forgotten the ghosts as he watched, so that his expectations, as she raised and lowered her arms, were quick with fear.

"It must be these folks he's staying wi," said Peerie. "They've made him different."

Chick whimpered: she had managed it, she had stepped out from behind the rock with her dress on, and he had seen no wonders.

Tom was standing by the edge of the sea.

CHAPTER
FIFTEEN

In the evening they stepped off the bus not far from the great derelict house. As soon as they entered the avenue Chick took from his pocket an apostle teaspoon and held it in his hand. Avenue and garden were a wilderness of willowherb, tall and red and aggressive, like gigantic cocks. Behind the house the hillside rose sheer, bristling with dark-leaved trees. The house itself was already in shadow, though sunshine still blazed on the Firth. It was so huge and so imposing on its eminence over the sea, that its glassless windows, its shattered roof, its dangling rone-pipes, and above all its open doors, made it look like an enormous sinister trap. Tables and striped deckchairs ought to have been on the lawn in front; shiny motor-cars on the carriage-way; rich people gazing out of the windows; and servants everywhere. Instead there was nobody but themselves, as they crept about reconnoitring. Chick tapped the walls with his spoon; it was like a kind of tuning-fork to which he listened as if to a warning. To Peerie he became the most uncanny thing in or out of the house. Peerie himself kept close to Tom; he would have held on to him if he had been allowed.

Upstairs they found a room whose ceiling was almost intact, and whose windows had some glass in them. The floor was littered with fallen plaster, withered leaves, and birds' dung.

"This could do," said Tom.

Chick was tapping his spoon against the marble fireplace.

"Are you trying to see if there's a secret passage, Chick?" asked Peerie.

Chick turned and tapped his brow with the spoon.

"I don't like it in here," he muttered.

Tom's smile now frightened Peerie as much as Chick's tapping did.

"I don't like it myself, Chick," he whispered.

"Why is it empty?" cried Chick. "Why did they go away and leave it?"

"If you meet them tonight ask them," said Tom, but in such a low voice that only Peerie heard.

"Listen," said Chick.

Outside on the road a car passed. In the garden a bird chirped. Transformed by Chick's listening, those sounds became strange and evil, from the world of ghosts. The terror was too much for Chick himself. He crouched down on the hearth, buried his head in his arms, and made noises of fear like an animal.

Peerie bravely went over to comfort him.

"There's nothing to be frightened aboot, Chick," he said. "It's just an empty hoose. The folk went away. Folk go away, Chick. Mind old Mr Camm went away and naebody knew where he went to?" Peerie groaned, having in his agitation of pity conjured up his own

158

private nightmare: Mr Camm's body had been dragged out of the Clyde months later. "Tom's no' frightened," he added.

But when he turned to look at Tom for reassurance he was again daunted by that smile, itself suggesting things which could not be seen.

"Chick's never been as bad as this before, Tom," he said. "It must be this hoose. Do you think it is haunted?"

"It's just haunted if you think it's haunted."

Peerie grinned; his eyes tried to keep out of the way of that unavoidable truth.

"I think we should sleep in the tent," he said. "For Chick's sake. He'll be a' right in the tent."

They stared at Chick who was now quiet; he still hid his face.

"My grannie says," whispered Peerie, "that one day he'll go like that and never get better. I hope it's no' this time. He's got his big knife wi' him. Poor Chick. He wasnae like this when he was wee."

"He's always been like this," said Tom.

"No, Tom, he was fine when he was wee. My grannie says it's in his family. He's got an uncle who's in an asylum." Peerie shuddered. "Will we go doon and put up the tent, Tom?"

"If you like."

"I think we should." Peerie spoke loudly to Chick. "Don't worry, Chick. We're no' going to sleep here. Tom and me's going to put up the tent ootside. It'll just be like camping."

"Come on then," said Tom.

"But we cannae leave Chick here by himself."

"He'll come after us. He's listening all the time."

As they were cautiously going down the broken stairs Peerie looked back and saw Chick slinking behind them.

Later, about eleven o'clock, they were lying in the tent which was pitched in a space cleared among the willowherb. Midges had tormented them while they were erecting it, and now the door-flap had had to be closed to keep them out. Peerie was playing his mouth organ, with monotonous melancholy. Chick killed midges and flies on the tent wall with his spoon. Tom stared at the roof.

Peerie shook the slavers out of his mouth organ. "Naebody's very cheery," he remarked.

Suddenly Tom swung over and caught Chick's wrist. "What time is it?" he asked. He looked at the watch himself. "Five to eleven." Then he lay down again.

"Sure Chick should keep that watch in his pocket?" said Peerie.

It had been taken from a jacket laid down by a boy playing football.

"Any cop seeing it would be suspicious," added Peerie.

Chick grinned and tapped the watch glass with his spoon.

"If you're caught," said Peerie, "we're a' caught."

In a sudden excitement Tom threw off the blanket and crawled to the door.

"Are you feeling sick again?" asked Peerie.

160

Tom said nothing but tried feverishly to untie the rope fastening the door-flap.

"Do you need to pee?" asked Peerie, with solicitous giggle.

Again he got no answer. Tom's frenzy of anger and impatience grew.

"I'll loosen it for you, Tom," said Peerie. "It was me that tied it."

But Tom tore up a part of the wall, pulling up pegs and ripping the canvas. Through the opening he slithered on his belly.

Peerie gawked out after him. "Where are you going, Tom?" he cried. "Can I come?"

Tom was already breaking through the willowherb.

"I'm coming," shouted Peerie, and went, all the faster because close behind him Chick came, too.

Reaching the road Tom ran along it, with the two others in desperate pursuit.

"Tom, Tom, don't leave me," shouted Peerie. "You know I'm frightened."

Chick just ran, saying nothing.

Tom halted and let them come up.

Peerie was as relieved as a dog that had found its master; his hand went about Tom's body and face, like a tongue. Tom struck it away.

Chick stood by, like a ghost.

"Where are you going, Tom?" begged Peerie. "Are you just going for a walk? I thought maybe you were going back to these people you were staying wi'."

"I'm never going back to them."

"That's whit I thought, Tom. Are you just oot for a walk?"

It was only just then that there occurred to Tom a way of relieving the agony of unrest and loneliness that had driven him out.

"I'm going to phone," he said.

"Who are you going to phone, Tom?"

"That's my business."

Peerie laughed, as if to signify that he himself had no business at all, but was willing to accept a share in anybody's.

"If you let me walk to the phone-box and back," he said, "I'll no' say a word the whole way."

"No."

Bats came out of the trees and flew about their heads. Chick shuffled a little nearer to the others. Peerie mumbled that bats' bites were poisonous; they ate toadstools, which were full of poison.

Tom set off, running in a resurgence of that anxiety which he knew was as insane as Chick's fit of fear in the empty house. He was running to phone and yet there was nothing to phone about. The connection between him and the Forbes family was broken, and could never be joined again. He was back where he belonged: the plan he had formed before leaving Glasgow could now be carried out. But he knew it never would be; whatever happened to him, he could not go back to his old life, he had left Donaldson's Court for ever.

Peerie trotted close behind, excited to garrulity by the bats. When the gulls wailed out on the darkened sea he thought it was the bats wailing, and began a long whimper to the night itself, for no one else listened, about how he preferred the city with its street lamps and many people; there no grass or trees or flowers grew, out of which came evil poisonous things like bats and toads, snakes and midges.

A bus approached from Dunroth and they had to stop and press close against the sea-dyke. It rushed past, brightly lit, on its way to Towellan; likely it was the last one there that night. Faces gazed out. A drunk man sang.

"I wish I was in it," said Peerie.

Then, for the sake of friendliness, forgetting how he had already been snubbed several times, he tried to get Tom to talk of these people he had been staying with. He knew their house would be bright and warm and cheerful, and if Tom liked both of them could, in imagination at least, enter it and so escape from this dark, lonely, inhospitable night. Tom stood at the threshold, barring the way; if he wanted he could coax Mrs Forbes to let him take Peerie back with him. Chick would have to sleep in the tent by himself; he couldn't be trusted to behave in a proper house; he would dirty things, he would steal, he would keek through the key-hole of the lavatory.

"This Mrs Forbes, Tom," panted Peerie, "is she a big woman?"

Tom was about to snub him again more fiercely than ever when he felt a desire himself to talk about Mrs Forbes. He knew he should have killed that desire as he had killed the rabbit; but he could not.

"No, she's no' very big," he said.

Peerie was delighted with his success. His own mother had died when he was three; now, in describing Mrs Forbes, he was describing her.

At last Tom said: "Why are you talking aboot her, Peerie? She doesnae even know you're alive."

"Didn't you tell her aboot me, Tom?"

"No. She's got a son of her ain, and his name's no' Peerie."

"Mine isnae really Peerie. It's George. Whit's his name, Tom?"

"Alistair."

"There's a lassie too, isn't there? Whit's her name?"

"Don't talk aboot her."

"I was just asking her name, Tom."

"Don't. Don't say anything."

They turned a corner and in front of them was the lighted phone-box. Beyond it, across the water, a lighthouse flashed, once, twice. Seconds later it flashed again.

A young man was in the box, telephoning; his bicycle stood outside. He was laughing as he spoke and listened.

They sat on the low dyke, with the sea washing on rocks below.

Peerie was fascinated by the youth in the phone-box.

"Who's he talking to?" he whispered. "I know. He's talking to his lass. She's got fair hair and she works in a big hotel." He built up a fantasy about that girl, how she would be busy putting hot-water bags in beds, and how she would have to go in and out of dozens of bedrooms, all with red carpets and red quilts.

164

Only the sea answered him, murmuring like a mother to a child garrulous with weariness and fear.

At last the young man came out. Mounting his bicycle, he pedalled past them. He was whistling.

For the first time since leaving the tent Chick spoke: "He's got nae lights."

Peerie gazed after the cyclist, hoping he came to no harm from car or bat or cliff or policeman.

Tom made for the kiosk. They hurried after him, hopeful to be allowed in; but he shut the door upon them. They pressed their faces against the glass.

He took out his money, to find he had only two pennies. Peerie at once took one from his pocket and tapped on the glass with it.

After a long hesitation Tom opened the door wide enough to take the penny.

"If you'd let me in," pleaded Peerie, "I wouldnae say a word. I wouldnae even listen if you didnae want me to."

Without heeding Tom closed the door again, and began to look up the directory. He knew McDaid was the name of the people who usually lived in the cottage. There was a McDaid with a Towellan number.

As he dropped the pennies in the box he kept Peerie's to the last. He grudged even that intrusion, and when he glanced at Peerie's face, with its nose flattened like an ape's, it was as if all Donaldson's Court waited outside.

It was Mrs Forbes who answered. "Towellan 1173," she said. "Mrs Forbes speaking." She sounded tired and unhappy.

He turned as still as the instrument in his hand; he could not speak; he had gone back to his own country, and had forgotten the language of hers.

"Who is it?" she asked.

He tried desperately to remember what could be said.

"Who's there?" she asked irritably. "Have you got the wrong number?"

"It's me: Tom Forbes." So difficult had been the effort to speak, he did not notice his mistake until he heard her cry, "Tom Forbes? Who's he?"

His blood turned chill with strangeness. "I mean, Tom Curdie," he said; but it was really that mythical person, Tom Forbes, he still thought he was.

Outside Peerie, more than ever like an ape, was grimacing congratulation.

It was now Mrs Forbes's turn to be silent. "So it's you, Tom?" she said at last. "Where have you been? Mr Forbes has been in Dunroth looking for you. He's just got back. He'll be down in a minute to speak to you."

He must have been in the bus that had passed.

"Where are you speaking from?" she asked. "Glasgow?"

"No."

She sighed with disappointment. "I thought you must have, even though you left your case. You had it packed."

"Yes."

"Why? Did you mean to go home?"

"I don't know, Mrs Forbes."

She was silent again; she did not know his language just as he did not know hers.

"Well, did you win?" she asked. "At the singing."

"No."

"Here's Mr Forbes; he'll talk to you."

Forbes, too, sounded weary and depressed. "So you've turned up?"

"Yes, sir."

"What have you been up to? You didn't sing this afternoon."

"No, sir."

"I've been in Dunroth looking for you. I saw the man who runs the singing competition. He told me you ran away before it was your turn. Why did you? You made a terrible fuss about getting in to sing, and then when you're given permission you don't sing and stay away for hours. You can't treat people that way, Tom, and expect them to respect and like you."

"I'm sorry, sir."

"Well, I suppose that's always something, provided it's genuine. Where are you speaking from?"

"A telephone-box between Dunroth and Towellan."

"Were you walking back? Have you spent all your money?"

Then Tom heard Mrs Forbes speaking to her husband.

"Yes, that's so, Mary," said Forbes. "Well, Tom, you can't stay out all night and sleep in the bracken, so you'll have to come back, for tonight anyway."

Outside the kiosk Peerie was being pestered by Chick who was embracing him.

Tom was in despair. What would be the good of going back even for one night? That feeling, which he could not control, of being among his own family, would immediately grow again, made more terrifying by the knowledge that Mr and Mrs Forbes, and perhaps Gillian, too, now saw him as a creature like Chick, sent into their home to cause trouble and create unhappiness.

Mrs Forbes spoke: "Did you hear what Mr Forbes said?"

"Yes, Mrs Forbes."

"Then don't let's have any more nonsense about it. You can't stay out and be picked up by the police. You've got enough sense to know we're responsible for you. Are you just trying to worry us by ringing us up and then not telling us what you're going to do?"

"No, no."

"It looks like it, Tom. What are you going to do?"

Outside Peerie and Chick were still scuffling. What he could not do, ever, was to go back with them.

"I'll come," he said.

"All right. How long do you think it'll take you?"

"About half an hour."

"There will be some supper waiting for you." Then she set down the telephone.

When he stepped out into the road Peerie rushed and seized him.

"Tell Chick he's to leave me alane," he sobbed.

Tom pulled the frantic hands away. "You've got to look after yourself, Peerie," he said. "I'm not going back wi' you."

Peerie's alarm and astonishment were prodigious. He could not express it in words; his hands scraped about his mouth like an imbecile baby's; and his big top-shaped head, with its coloured cap, seemed to swell with the pressure of horror in it.

Chick crept up. "We don't need him, Peerie," he chuckled. "You and me will get on fine."

"No, I'm frightened of you, Chick," cried Peerie; then he began to shriek as Tom ran off into the dark: "Don't leave me, Tom, I wouldnae hae come if it hadnae been for you. I'll sleep ootside the door."

But he could not go racing after Tom: Chick held him fast.

Mingled with Peerie's shrieks were the wailings of a nightbird. Across the sea flashed the lighthouse, and now above the hills rose the moon. As Tom ran he felt that what he was hurrying towards kept receding. When he reached the cottage it would be there, gleaming in the moonlight under the trees, and he would be able to enter it easily, for the door would not be locked; but when he entered, and Mrs and Mrs Forbes were watching him eat his supper, this feeling of unattainableness would become a terror, worse than any ghost that might haunt Chick and Peerie's tent that night. He would be amidst what he wanted, and yet never be able to obtain it.

Once, suffocated in mind by that foreboding, he had to stop and lean against the dyke. He could no longer hear Peerie, but the bird still wailed, and somehow both the beam of the lighthouse and the moon in the sky seemed within easy reach. If he wanted he could have stretched out and taken them, as he might a wild rose from a bush. He did not want them; what he wanted was nearer, much nearer, but it could never be had.

CHAPTER
SIXTEEN

After Tom had had supper and gone to bed Mary and Charlie, in purged voices, like strangers talking, had discussed what should be done with him. Before he had gone out of the room Mary had stopped him at the door and asked if he wanted to stay with them for a few days longer or would prefer to go home immediately. After a long pause, during which Mary found herself praying he would not shed tears, he had nodded and said he would like to stay. Had he wept his strangeness, already repelling, would have become unbearable. Luckily he hadn't. Mary had said they would see.

"Well, Mary," said Charlie, "it was you who asked him."

"Do you object?"

"Oh no, no."

"It's not for his sake," she said. "It's for Gillian's. I don't think it would help her if he went tomorrow."

"You mean, she's got to be given a chance to make amends?"

"I mean nothing of the kind." But she could not have explained what she did mean: between Gillian and this strange boy had grown a relationship which must either be quite dissolved or else made comprehensible before he left them for good. If he were to go tomorrow Gillian might brood for the rest of the holiday; in her own way she too could be unfathomable.

"As you wish, Mary." His smile of capitulation had slipped; in a hurry, as visibly and pathetically as an old man his glasses, he set it to rights again. Only then did he dare to look straight at her. "So that's us on an even keel again?" he asked.

"I hope so. But we'll see."

"I suppose," he said timidly, "Gillian's at a temperamental age. The mind's a strange world."

She was in no humour for his philosophising, especially in such a defeated tone. "It's after twelve," she said. "I'm going to bed."

"But she's not an invalid," he added, in the same tone, but with the slightest hint of rebellion. "She's not ill."

She knew what he was hinting at: since Tuesday she had slept with Gillian, he with Alistair. She knew, too, he thought he was being excluded as a punishment, and in his present mood of humility could not protest.

"I thought you believed the troubles of the mind are harder to cure than those of the flesh," she said.

He submitted, with a sigh.

"And we're going to Rothesay tomorrow afternoon, if it's dry?" she asked, at the door.

"Yes, by all means."

"You don't sound very keen, Charlie. I thought you never regarded the holiday as complete without at least one pilgrimage to Canada Hill."

172

He winced at her mockery. "It's only a place with a fine viewpoint," he murmured.

"You're learning, Charlie," she said, and went.

He sat for a little while examining those fresh lacerations on his soul. In time no doubt she would again sheathe her claws, as she had done for so many years; but she had used them and would in future not be so reluctant to use them again. Let him nurture another white doe, and out the claws would spring. Indeed, had he not, by a master-stroke of irony, become a white doe himself, confined to the bare small circle of fact, and prevented from speeding through the green forests of imagination and hope and truth?

Perhaps, he thought, as he too made for bed, freedom might be gained for a little while on Canada Hill.

Next morning he volunteered to help Mary in the house so that an early start could be made after dinner.

"But you promised you'd go out in the boat with me, Pop," cried Alistair.

"It's about time," said his mother, "you stopped calling your father 'Pop'. I've been waiting to see when he was going to check you himself."

"I must say," said Mrs Storrocks, "I've been surprised at you, Charles, a teacher of English, allowing such slang."

"It's not the name that matters," he muttered, "it's the affection or lack of it with which it's said."

"Rubbish!" she cried.

So it was rubbish, of course. He had heard "bugger" used affectionately.

173

"Who'll go out with me, then?" asked Alistair. "You'll not let me go out by myself."

"No, we won't," said his mother. "Gillian will go with you."

Gillian nodded.

"That's not a very polite answer," said her mother sharply.

"Yes, I'll go, Mummy," she said at once, with excessive politeness.

"But she'll not let me row," protested Alistair.

"Yes, she will," said his mother. "What about you, Tom?"

He looked at Gillian who stared stonily back. "I'll just go for a walk up the hill," he said.

"You'll do nothing of the kind," said Mrs Storrocks.

"I'm dealing with this, Mother," said Mary.

Gillian looked at her mother; she was evidently willing to have Tom with her, but only if asked; she would not offer.

"I don't want any carry-on," said Mary.

"I'm sure if there is," snapped Mrs Storrocks, "Tom won't be the cause of it."

Mary looked out of the window at the sea. "I don't know if I should let any of you go." Then she turned irritably to Charlie. "You're in charge of the boating."

"The sea's calm, Mary. The sun's shining. As your mother said, there will be no danger if there's no silliness."

"I didn't ask for a sermon. So you think they should go?"

"Yes. Gillian's as good with the oars as I am. In any case," he added, raising his head, "faith is buoyant."

174

Mrs Storrocks laughed. "There are times when I think I'm in a Chinese house."

"Off you go then," said Mary to the children. "Don't go far out, and if it gets rough come in at once."

"When I was Gillian's age," said Mrs Storrocks, "I could row from here to Dunroth and back before breakfast. Before breakfast," she repeated, and went out, almost dancing.

Alistair scowled after her. "Why can't she row now?" he asked.

"No cheek," said his mother. When she had seen them out she went into the kitchen.

Alone in the room, Charlie watched the children go down to the beach. Alistair raced on ahead, Tom walked quickly, Gillian dawdled.

"It must be buoyant," he muttered, "otherwise how in God's name do we stay afloat?"

Turning to the table he began to clear it. He was on his way into the kitchen with a pile of dishes so high and precarious that carrying it was a test of faith. A cup fell and was smashed.

Mary ran through. "For God's sake, Charlie," she screamed, "be more careful."

He gaped down at the fragments. "It's just a white breakfast cup, Mary, easily replaced."

She turned her back and uttered moans either of threat or despair.

"You think everything's easily replaced," she said, and again he couldn't be sure whether she was threatening or despairing.

When he crept round she hid her face in her apron.

"I do think, Mary," he whispered, "there's nothing broken between us that can't be mended."

"I'll go up and make the beds," she said. "You can clear up here if you want to."

She rushed away. He knew she would lie on their bed and weep. They were not yet on an even keel.

The sink was filled with warm suddy water ready for the dishes. As he stood over it, aproned, with his sleeves rolled up, he lifted a saucer and, gently settling it on the water, watched it float; like faith, it was buoyant. Then he poured a little water into it, and a little more. Slowly it sank and soon could not be seen through the suds. Did faith too sink so readily, and disappear?

Taking advantage of Gillian's aloofness, Alistair appointed himself captain. He it was who pushed least and bragged most in launching the boat; he was first in and seized the oars; and he ordered Tom and Gillian to sit together in the stern, but he did not insist when she stepped past him to sit by herself at the bow. His first few strokes were clumsy through eagerness and took the boat round in a circle, but soon, inspired by his own gasped encouragements, he was rowing steadily up the coast towards Towellan Pier.

"We'll not go all the way," he panted.

"You couldn't," said Gillian; she had her back to him and Tom, and gazed down into the water.

"I could," he cried indignantly. "Easily. Couldn't I, Tom?"

"How does he know? He's a stranger."

"He's seeing me now, isn't he?"

176

"Yes, but he's saying nothing, as usual. Suppose we bump into a basking shark?"

He laughed, but glanced about nervously. "There aren't any."

"There were last year." She paused, staring down at the seaweed on the sunlit sandy seabed; there she saw a fish smaller than her little finger. "As big as elephants," she said.

"So they were."

"Remember how you yelled to be put ashore, because there was one too near the boat?"

"Oh, what a lie, Gillian! I didn't yell."

"Howled then."

"And I didn't howl either. She's just making it up, Tom."

"Yes," she said, as if talking to the sea. "I just make things up."

"I wasn't frightened really, Tom. But all the other boats were going ashore. Daddy said they weren't dangerous, but Mummy wouldn't believe him."

Looking up, Gillian noticed somebody on the beach; he seemed to be keeping pace with them and waving. He was a boy, and boys often were friendly when they hoped for a favour, such as a row in the boat; but this seemed a boy different from the rest she had met at Towellan.

Tom wasn't listening to Alistair's account of the basking sharks. He had noticed Gillian's interest in the boy on shore; and he had already recognised that boy as Peerie.

She turned round.

"Who's he waving to?" she asked.

"Who?" Alistair twisted round. "He'll just want into the boat. Maybe he thinks I'm a good rower."

"He's shouting 'Tom'," said Gillian.

They listened. "Tom! Tom!" shouted Peerie, as he stumbled along the shore.

"So it is you," she said. "Is he a friend of yours?"

"No."

"You don't seem very sure." Then, to Alistair's annoyance, she became the keen-eyed sharp-voiced skipper. "Row nearer the shore," she ordered. "Make for those rocks."

He obeyed, pointing out how to row near rocks needed skill and nerve.

Gillian was watching Peerie keenly, as if he was some aborigine whom the expedition was seeing for the first time.

"Is he human?" she asked. "Or is he a kind of seal?"

Eager to meet the boat, Peerie was creeping out to it over green slimy rocks.

"Watch him fall in," said Gillian. "Isn't he a freak?"

Peerie wore his coloured jockey cap and his jeans with the cowboys. His face, twisted in sycophantic grimaces, was tearstained and sorrowful. Crouched on the rock, with the sea lapping about him, he was like some sea-creature dressed up to do tricks.

Gillian reached out and manoeuvred the boat between two rocks, where it rested. An oar could have touched Peerie.

He grinned at Tom in shame and entreaty.

"I'll see if he understands English," said Gillian. "Hello. Who are you?"

Embarrassed and puzzled, he looked to Tom for guidance. Left to himself, he did what he always dangerously did, fell back on the truth. "George Whitehouse," he replied. "But my nickname's Peerie."

"Peerie? A peerie's a top." Then she saw the resemblance and laughed. "It's a good nickname," she said. "Did Tom give it to you?"

Again he appealed to Tom. "I don't know," he muttered. "I've had it a long time."

"But you've known Tom a long time, haven't you?"

"For years. Sure that's right, Tom?"

"Tom says he doesn't know you."

In his consternation Peerie put one hand on his heart and held the other up to heaven.

"Do you come from Glasgow?" asked Gillian.

He nodded. Although he kept answering her it was Tom he looked at all the time. Tom did not look away always, but it was when he looked at him that Peerie felt most denied.

"Do you live beside Tom?" asked Gillian. "In the place called Donaldson's Court?"

He pleaded with her. "Aye, up the next close. Whit's wrang wi' Tom? Has he got a sore throat? Can he no' speak?"

"Oh, he can speak all right. But he doesn't know you, so why should he speak to you?"

"But he does know me. I was talking to him last night, me and Chick."

"Chick? Who's he? Is he another one of your gang?"

Peerie nodded.

"What does your gang do? Does it break into shops, or does it just lift things from counters?"

Peerie realised her friendliness was a trap.

"I'm no' going to say onything," he muttered.

"But if Tom won't talk to you, you should be pleased that I do."

"Tom," he cried. "I've got to talk to you. You ken who it's aboot."

"Chick?" asked Gillian.

"I'm no' talking to you."

"You might as well, for Tom's not hearing a word you say."

"He is. He's no' deef. It's just because you're here. If you werenae here he'd talk to me. Sure that's right, Tom?"

"Where are you staying in Towellan?" asked Gillian.

Again her friendly tone tempted him. "In a tent."

"Where have you got it pitched?"

He waved in the direction of Dunroth.

"How long have you been here?"

"We just came yesterday."

"Was it all arranged between you and Tom?"

That arrangement was proof of his friendship with Tom; he could not deny it.

"I see," she murmured, smiling and paddling her hand in the water.

Alistair was bored. "I came out to row," he muttered.

Gillian kept smiling and paddling. Peerie kept appealing in vain to Tom.

"Should I push her out, Gillian?" whispered Alistair.

"Unless Tom has something to say to his friend," she said.

180

Alistair looked at Tom uneasily; he did not like that queer silence. "Nobody wants to say anything," he said, "so I think we'll go."

Gillian helped him to push the boat out.

As it moved away Peerie began to weep. He made to jump on to another rock further out and slithered into the water, up to his waist.

Those in the boat weren't sure which way he would start wading.

"If he's not careful," said Alistair, "he'll get drowned."

Disconsolately, Peerie turned and waded ashore.

"Silly ass," commented Alistair, now rowing strongly again.

Gillian sat straight and stared past her brother at Tom.

"Do you know what I hate most of all?" she asked.

Alistair liked such games. "In the whole world?"

"Yes, in the whole world."

"Scrambled eggs?" he suggested, with a chuckle.

"Don't be stupid. Something important."

He could think of nothing more important than food, except perhaps blisters, for there was one forming on his right palm.

"I give in," he said.

"A traitor. Somebody who says he doesn't know his friends."

Alistair understood; he gave Tom a comradely smile; they were both sufferers from Gillian's criticisms.

"If I'd been Tom," he said, "I wouldn't have wanted to talk to him. He was a silly ass. I could have had a cap like yon, only mummy wouldn't let me."

"What's the matter with your right hand?" asked Gillian. "You're not rowing straight."

"I've got a blister." He paused in his rowing to look at it; it was big enough to justify squint rowing, indeed it justified letting someone else row for a change. "It's a big one, a whopper."

"Let Tom row," she said.

He agreed eagerly. Compared with Gillian's his own rowing would not have looked much, but compared with Tom's it would look excellent.

"Careful when you're changing places," she said.

"Do you want to row?" asked Alistair.

Tom nodded. "I'll try," he said. But the reason was that he would have his back to Gillian.

As they went up to the house after they had beached the boat, Gillian asked Tom casually: "Do you want us to say nothing about meeting your friend Peerie?"

He moved his head.

"What does that mean?" she asked and, laughing, ran across to where the putters had been left lying on the grass. "I'm going to have a game of putting before dinner."

"I can't," said Alistair, holding up his right hand with a hand-kerchief wrapped round it. "I'm going in to see if dinner's ready."

He ran into the house, with his injured hand ready to show. He would tell his mother about it, and about Peerie.

"What about you?" asked Gillian, of Tom. "Do you want to play?"

He shook his head.

"I forgot you can't speak," she said, and putted the ball towards the first hole. It was a good shot, and she was in in two. When she looked up she saw Tom watching her as if he was about to speak. So strongly did she get that impression that she waited; but when he remained silent, she laughed, and went on with her game.

Alistair found his mother in the dining-room setting the table.

"Well, did you have a nice row?" she asked.

He made his bandaged hand conspicuous. "Oh yes, thanks."

"What's the matter with your hand?"

"Oh, it's just a blister."

"Let me see it."

Tenderly he removed the handkerchief. She glanced and smiled.

"You'll not die," she said, and went on with her work.

"It's jolly sore."

"Where's Gillian?"

"She's putting." He picked an apple from the bowl on the sideboard.

"Not before your dinner."

He grumbled as he put it down. "When will it be ready?"

"It won't be long. Did you reach the pier?"

"Nearly."

"Did you see anything interesting on your voyage?"

"No. Oh yes, lots of things: a dead jellyfish as big as a parasol; a bald man in swimming; and we met a friend of Tom's."

She paused, on the point of placing a fork on the table. "A friend of Tom's?"

"Well, he said he was, but Tom said he wasn't. It was a lot of nonsense really. Tom wouldn't talk to him. Gillian did, though. She asked him lots of things."

"Where was this?"

"He was on the beach and he shouted to us." He laughed. "You should have seen the way he was dressed, Mummy. He had a jockey's cap all coloured, like the kind you wouldn't let me have; and he had yellow cowboys on his trousers. He had a big funny head. Gillian said he was a freak. He's staying in a tent. He said they had a gang that stole things from shops."

"Alistair, you and Gillian haven't made this up between you?"

"No, Mummy. Ask Gillian."

"And Tom just sat in the boat and said nothing?"

"That's right. He didn't say a single word. What's for the dinner, Mum? I'm hungry."

Quietly his mother finished the arrangement of the cutlery.

"Alistair, I want you to go and tell Gillian to come."

"Has she to help?"

"Yes."

"She'll be mad, because she'll be in the middle of a game." He departed, pleased to get this small revenge for her teasing him about his fear of the basking sharks.

"Charlie," called Mary.

"Yes, dear," came his voice from the kitchen.

"Come here a minute."

He came in, still wearing his apron and carrying a fork in his hand; he had been testing the potatoes with it.

"Another five minutes should see them ready," he said. "Was that Ferdinand Magellan I heard returned?"

"Yes."

"Safe and sound?"

"Except for a blister on his hand. But he brought strange news."

"Can you return from new worlds without strange news?"

"It's about Tom."

"Oh."

"It may just be some of Alistair's nonsense," said Mary. "I've sent out for Gillian. But whatever it is, Charlie, we're going to discuss it like sane people."

"Like man and wife, I hope."

"Like sane people. Alistair says that when they were out in the boat they met a friend of Tom's from Glasgow. From Alistair's description a queer-looking creature."

"He must have been. Was he squatted on a rock, out in the sea, like a seal?"

"Are you making a fool of me, Charlie?"

"No, no. But you must admit out in a rowing boat's a funny place to meet anybody."

"Funny or not," she yelled, "they met him. And do you know what he told them? He told them he was a member of a gang that stole things from shops."

He had switched on his surrender smile, but it now became agitated. "First they meet him in the sea, and then, gratutiously, he confesses he's one of a gang of thieves. Now be fair, Mary. Doesn't it sound like something out of one of Alistair's storybooks?"

"It was your son who said it, Charlie. Is he a liar, too, like your daughter?"

"Well, Mary, Gillian did admit she lied, or as I prefer to call it, romanced."

"Don't give it any of your fancy names. Lied. But did she? Did she?"

"It was yourself who told me, Mary."

"But has it never occurred to you that she might have decided to lie about it for your sake?"

"You mean, she did see him steal?"

"Yes, that's what I mean."

"She accused him, and then falsely withdrew her accusation?"

"You're beginning to see what's been blazing in your eyes."

"You must admit, Mary, I did think of it."

"And I've thought of nothing else."

"But you've not been sure, Mary?"

"How could I be, when every night she sticks to her story?"

There was a knock at the door, and Gillian came in, cool and grave.

"Alistair said you wanted me to help, Mummy."

"What we want you to do, Gillian, is to tell us the truth about this queer story Alistair's brought home about meeting a friend of Tom's."

Gillian nodded, and spoke with pedantic precision. "We were out in the boat when a boy shouted 'Tom'. Tom said he didn't know him, but we rowed over to him; he came to meet us very anxiously. He said his name was Peerie; I forget his other name. His head was

186

shaped like a peerie. He was dressed in a coloured cap and blue jeans with yellow cowboys sewn on to them. He wasn't very intelligent. He said he came from Donaldson's Court. He's living in a tent along the Dunroth road, with somebody else called Chick. He said that their coming here to stay in the tent was arranged before Tom came to stay with us. Tom didn't speak to him once, though he was desperate to get Tom to speak to him. He said he wanted to tell Tom something about Chick. That was all, Mummy."

"Are you sure?"

Gillian reflected. "I think so."

"According to Alistair, he said he was a member of a gang that stole things from shops. Did he?"

Gillian judicially shook her head. "No. He said he was a member of a gang, but he didn't admit they stole things from shops."

"Alistair said he did."

"No, Mummy, he didn't."

Her father spoke, humbly. "Did you ask him if he stole things from shops?"

"Yes, Daddy."

"Wasn't that an odd question to ask somebody you've just met for the first time?"

Gillian did not reply. She gazed out of the window where Alistair was trying to putt with his left hand. Tom wasn't to be seen.

"Wasn't it, Gillian?" asked her father again.

"Yes, Daddy."

"This idea of stealing's in your head, Gillian. What put it there?" He took hold of her gently by the shoulders. "Gillian, did you see Tom stealing in Woolworth's last Tuesday? I want the truth."

She would not look towards her mother for help or sympathy.

"Did you, Gillian?"

"Yes," she cried, "yes, I saw him. But I don't know what he did it for."

"I don't think that matters, to us. The important thing as far as I'm concerned, Gillian, is that I've found out that you love me more than truth. I'm not going to find fault with you for that, whoever else may." He kissed her on the brow.

"I hate him," she whispered, "I hate him."

"I don't think you should. Hate what he does, when it's wrong, like stealing, or lying, but try not to hate him."

"I do hate him."

Her mother put her arm round her. "Never mind, Gillian. It's over now. We'll send him away and forget him. He's not worth hating. It looks as though he's had it all arranged, to bring his pals down with him. You go and tell the others dinner's ready. Your grandma said she was going for a stroll on the beach, but you'll likely find her on her way up. As you know, she smells when the food's ready." She smiled at that family joke.

Gillian did not smile.

"By Jove, she'll have no trouble smelling the potatoes," cried her father, rushing into the kitchen. "They're burnt to cinders," he sang out.

Mary sniffed as the lid came off. "They certainly are. Now off you go, Gillian."

"Are we still going to Rothesay?" asked Gillian.

"Do you want to?"

"Yes."

"All right, we'll go."

"Will he go with us?"

"Do you mean Tom?"

"Yes."

"I don't know, Gillian. I'll have to see your father about it."

"I want him to go." Then Gillian went quickly away.

Her mother, shaking her head in perplexity, hurried into the kitchen. It was full of steam, the stench of burnt potatoes, and Charlie's laughter.

She could not help laughing herself. "What are they like?"

He waved the pot under her nose. "Just the way your mother likes them."

The tears in her eyes were not altogether caused by the steam. "Oh, Charlie!" she cried.

With the pot in one hand he embraced her with the other. "No use crying over burnt potatoes, my dear; or a failed experiment."

"We'll get rid of him tomorrow," she said. "You'll have to see him on the steamer to make sure he doesn't sneak off to stay with these pals of his."

"I'll take him the whole way home."

"Maybe it would be as well, Charlie. When are you going to tell him? And what are you going to tell him? You could say we've got somebody coming unexpectedly and the hut's needed."

"He'll be told, Mary."

"When he's gone we'll maybe all be able to understand one another again."

"And your mother won't feel she's living in a Chinese house."

They both laughed, but they knew in their hearts, she in her way and he in his, that love had failed amongst them, and for the rest of their lives they, and their children, must live in the shadow of that failure.

Then Mrs Storrocks came in, lamenting the burnt potatoes.

CHAPTER
SEVENTEEN

Mary's gaiety that afternoon affected her family, so that Tom's isolation among them became more marked. She did not intend that effect, but noticed it without much compunction; indeed, it was a faint but stubborn sense of guilt towards him, as well as towards Charlie, that caused her to express her happiness and relief with such ostentation.

It was a brilliant, warm afternoon when they got off the bus at Towellan Pier. The steamer which was to take them to Rothesay was already in sight.

"Well, we're in good time," she said, "thanks to you, Charlie."

He knew also her gaiety was partly false: it could not be otherwise, so soon after that revelation; perhaps, indeed, her happiness, like his own, never had been quite genuine, and never could be. Nevertheless, in loyalty and affection, and as a sharer of the burden, he laughed, too, and jested, glancing down to see if he still wore his apron.

They were approaching the gate on to the pier when Alistair seized his mother's arm. "See," he hissed, "that's him, over there, Tom's friend, Peerie."

Peeping round the corner of a boatshed was a boy peculiar in more than his dress. Gillian had said he wasn't very intelligent; to Mary he seemed a half-wit. Though he obviously did not want to be seen by them he just as obviously couldn't keep out of sight. His antics and his coloured cap reminded her of a chimpanzee she had once seen at the zoo; it had hopped about in some kind of subhuman excitement just like this. Then she realised he must be trying to attract Tom's attention, while at the same time avoiding theirs.

She walked over to Tom. "Is that a friend of yours?" she asked pleasantly.

He had already seen Peerie. "No, Mrs Forbes."

"Are you sure? Alistair told me you've met him today already. He certainly seems to think he knows you."

"I used to know him."

It was a strange answer, strangely spoken. Boys, she supposed, fell out as girls did; she wondered what had caused it.

"He thinks he still knows you."

"What's wrong?" asked Mrs Storrocks.

"Nothing, Mother. Tom's just seen a boy who's a neighbour of his in Glasgow."

"Good gracious! Where is he?"

As if to oblige her Peerie, in his full freakishness, had come out from behind the shed. He still gesticulated, but without confidence.

"His trousers are wet," said Alistair, laughing. "He fell in this morning, up to here."

"What a creature!" said his grandmother. "I hope, Tom, you keep him at a distance."

"I don't think you need worry about that, Mother," said Mary.

Charlie had been chatting to Bob Moodie at the gate. "Come on, you people," he called. "Do you want to miss the steamer? All paid for here."

They filed past Bob with his satchel.

"A grand day," he said.

"Isn't it?" agreed Mary cheerfully.

"No day's grand enough for daylight robbery," snorted Mrs Storrocks.

"What a surprise you're going to get, Mrs Storrocks," said her son-in-law, "when you arrive at the gates of heaven and find there's a toll to pay."

"So you've got me dead, Charles? You forget that that toll is being paid here and now, daily."

"I don't forget that," he murmured.

Mary was laughing at this exchange between her mother and husband when Alistair caught her by the cardigan.

"He's coming, Mummy. He's on the pier."

They all looked back to see Peerie safely past Bob Moodie.

"Who in heaven's name is he?" asked Charlie.

"That's him," Mary whispered, "Tom's friend. He seems to be interested in us."

Charlie could not share her amusement. He scowled and muttered what sounded to her like "scum of the earth". It was a judgment that might have been her mother's. She could not help laughing.

"What if he follows us to Rothesay?" asked Alistair, thrilled.

"He won't," said his father grimly.

"But how could you stop him, Dad?"

"I shall see to it that he pesters none of us." He included Tom in his protective glower.

"If the creature's got its fare," said Mrs Storrocks, "then it's entitled to go to Rothesay, like anybody else."

"He's not entitled to make himself a nuisance by following people about," said Charlie.

"I wouldn't heed him," whispered Mary. "I don't think he's all there."

"It won't be very pleasant having an imbecile following us around, especially dressed like that."

"No, Charlie," she said, and did not laugh.

Then the steamer came in, the gangway was hoisted, and the little group of Towellan people went on board. Peerie darted on last, just as the men were untying the ropes from the gangway.

"He's coming," said Alistair, in glee. "I bet he's going to try and skip it." He was by no means shocked; he seemed to think that to be able to travel without paying showed resource, wisdom, economy, and daring.

Charlie and Mary exchanged glances, hers proud and content, his sombre; but each glance admitted the same thing, that their own son, if he had been taken from them at birth and brought up in Donaldson's Court, would have turned out to be no more honest than Tom and Peerie.

Then Mary had to go with her mother to find seats in the sun and out of the wind. Charlie went below with Alistair to look at the engines.

Gillian remained on deck. Not far from her Tom, at the rail, gazed so earnestly shorewards she thought he was like an emigrant going to some country like New Zealand, thousands of miles away, from which he might never return. Rothesay, of course, was only half an hour's sailing away.

Now that the two women and the man were gone, Peerie crept out of hiding. On his way to Tom he passed Gillian without noticing her. When she said "Hello" he gave a whimper of fright, and then a grin of apology and entreaty mixed.

"I've got to talk to Tom," he explained.

"You're very persistent," she said.

He wasn't sure what she meant. "It's important," he muttered.

"Well, there he is, at the rail."

"I can see him. Will he talk to me noo?"

"I don't think so. But you can try."

"But whit will he no' talk to me for?"

"I don't know." She really did not know; it seemed to her that the obvious explanations, shame and fear, were inadequate. "You'll just have to try. Is it about Chick?"

He could not keep an expression of horror from contorting his face.

"What has he done?" she asked. "It must have been something terrible."

He nodded. "I cannae tell you. I can just tell Tom."

"But what if he doesn't listen to you? You've got to tell somebody, haven't you? You can tell me if you like; that's to say, if Tom'll not listen."

Shaking his head doubtfully, Peerie slunk off to try. He couldn't help liking her freckled cheerfulness, even though when she was in the boat that morning she had made a fool of him.

He couldn't get into the rail close to Tom. There was a man at one side and a stout woman at the other; both looked as if they would object if he tried to squeeze in. He had to poke Tom in the back. Tom turned, saw him, but pretended not to: it was as if the poke had been done by a stranger accidentally. Peerie was so disconcerted by that stare that for a moment or two he wondered if this boy in the clean jerkin and khaki shorts really was Tom Curdie, who lived beside him in Donaldson's Court in Glasgow, and who for years had been kind to him.

What was in his mind was red-hot. He grabbed Tom's jerkin and tugged. "I've got to talk to you, Tom," he whispered. "It's aboot Chick."

The woman turned and made a red, go-away face.

Tom still looked towards the shore; but he was not seeing the trees and hills, or even the white lighthouse; he was remembering the house in Donaldson's Court, and comparing his mother there with Mrs Forbes.

"Oh, go away," said the woman, again. "You're a nuisance."

That was what Peerie wanted, to go away with Tom to a corner below, beside the engines, where it was darker and the noise would make the telling of his awful news about Chick less dangerous.

"Come on, Tom," he urged.

196

"Didn't you hear me?" asked the woman. "You're a nuisance."

He had to stand back, thwarted. When he turned he saw the girl waving at him; there was nothing he could do but wave back sadly.

Then he tried again and this time dislodged the stout woman. Really the position was now too breezy for her.

"I can see I'll get no peace here," she said.

She had a camera round her neck and a bag on her arm. As he looked after her Peerie felt like shouting she was lucky she hadn't spoken to Chick like that, for he'd have stolen her camera or said rude things about her fat bum.

He burrowed in close to Tom.

"Do you know what he's done this time, Tom?" he whispered. "This is the worst ever."

Tom seemed more interested in a gull flying steadfastly above their heads. Peerie didn't like its yellow sinister eye. Before he could go on and tell Tom about Chick, the ship's band, a fiddle and an accordion, arrived to play behind them. People sang to the cheerful music. A young couple danced two or three light-hearted steps. Peerie was annoyed, until he realised that the music would be as good as the noise of the engines to protect his secret.

Tom wondered what it was Chick had done. Had he stolen something valuable, or had he attacked a girl in some lonely place?

"You're no' listening, Tom," whined Peerie. "I cannae tell you if you don't listen. It isnae fair. I wouldnae hae come if it hadnae been for you. I'll tell my grannie."

"Go hame," said Tom, and walked quickly away.

With tears in his eyes Peerie gaped after him. "Hame?" he repeated stupidly, not knowing whether the word meant the tent or the cottage Tom was living in or Donaldson's Court.

The man with the little red bag jingled by for pennies for the band. Peerie put in a penny; it was really to pay for the company of all these other people who put pennies in too. But when the bag was past he felt more lonely than ever.

Some of those other people were smiling in sympathy at the faces of grief he was making, but he could not smile back. Then the band went away and a woman, scented, with her ringed hand holding a biscuit, came forward. He thought it was for him, and in spite of his terrible anxiety was going to accept it, for he felt hungry; but she stepped past and held it out to the gulls. One flew near but somehow pretended to be looking ahead, not at the biscuit at all, so that when it made its snatch, everybody, including Peerie, was startled. People laughed. Looking after the gull, which now flew close to the water, Peerie felt a kinship with it, for in a way it had eaten his biscuit. But it had plenty of other gulls to speak to.

Even when the steamer entered Rothesay Bay, where six submarines lay alongside their depot ship, he was not comforted. Other boys rushed to the rails, among them the Forbes boy Alistair. What Peerie noticed most of all was the sailors' washing on the depôt ship; it reminded him of the backcourts of home. He decided bitterly that when he grew up, and his grannie was dead, he would join the Navy and sail to some far-off place and never come back.

CHAPTER
EIGHTEEN

While they were standing outside Rothesay Pier to confer as to how they should spend the afternoon, Alistair caught sight of Peerie skulking behind a weighing-machine; he was still spying on them.

Charlie was furious. Resolute to protect the flawed happiness of his family, he could not see the humour of that absurd pursuit.

"What does he want?" he kept asking.

"He's lonely," said Gillian unexpectedly.

"Lonely?" Her father gazed round at the numerous holiday-makers.

"And he's got something he wants to tell Tom."

"How do you know?"

"He said so this morning, and he told me again on the steamer."

"Do you mean to tell me you spoke to that idiotic riff-raff on the steamer?"

"Yes, Daddy."

"In heaven's name, why?"

"I felt sorry for him."

"Sorry? Your pity does you credit, Gillian, but I assure you it's wasted on the likes of that. You keep back from him. God knows what filthy thoughts will swarm and spawn beneath that cap."

"I thought," said Mrs Storrocks, "we came to Rothesay for an afternoon's enjoyment."

"So we did," said Mary. "Well, Charlie, it's decided then. My mother and I will go for a look round the shops; you take the children up Canada Hill."

"That was my intention, Mary," he said, scowling towards Peerie, "but I don't relish being made a public laughing-stock. If he was a dog," he added, in a passion of frustration, "we could throw stones to discourage him."

His mother-in-law rebuked him. "The boy's a fool, Charles, but he's doing no harm."

"If Tom went over and spoke to him," suggested Gillian, "he might go away."

"No," said her mother. "I told Tom to keep back from him."

But Charlie was considering the idea. "If that's all he wants, just to tell Tom something, maybe it would be as well to let him do it."

Mary smiled and shrugged her shoulders. "I got the impression Tom didn't want to speak to him. But it's all the same to me."

They all looked at Tom. He shook his head.

"What does that mean?" demanded Charlie.

"It's plain enough to me," said Mrs Storrocks. "He doesn't want to have anything to do with him; and in my opinion he's quite right. Encourage that sort and they'll be pitching their tent on the lawn."

Mary couldn't help laughing at that grotesque possibility.

"No, they wouldn't," said Charlie. "There are such people as police. Well, Tom, are you going over to tell your friend to go away and leave us in peace?"

"I'd rather not, sir."

"Good heavens, what are you afraid of? He won't attack you. We'll see to that."

"They've fallen out," whispered Mary. "But don't ask me why."

"My God," he muttered, "are we being dragged into their squabbles next?"

"You didn't think, did you, Charlie, that when you brought Tom to Towellan you cut every connection between him and Donaldson's Court?"

It was asked as banter; but to Charlie it brought fresh revelation. There was no doubt he had not made the imaginative effort necessary to appreciate Tom's difficulties in resisting his environment; and there could be no doubt either that he hadn't made that effort because he could not: his compassion was academic, as Todd had said, not creative; and his love was cowardly.

"We'll meet you here at five," said Mary, "and then we'll all go for tea. Have a nice time."

He smiled and waved after her. Already she was laughing merrily.

"Come on," he said, and set off.

"Are we going to take the bus, Dad?" asked Alistair anxiously.

"We are not." Charlie laughed. He suddenly felt lighter in heart; truth, as well as faith, was buoyant.

202

"But I'm sweating already."

"Pilgrims must walk and sweat and arrive weary."

"I'm not a pilgrim."

"No, son, none of us is. But it is good to remember that hundreds of years ago, in the so-called barbaric ages, they walked thousands of miles, across mountains and deserts, through lands infested with robbers and murderers, to reach the holy shrine."

"They hadn't any buses in those days," said Alistair.

"No, they hadn't." It was difficult to know what to say next. He solved it by turning to Gillian. "You'd rather walk, wouldn't you, Gillian?"

"Yes, Daddy."

"Look at the long legs she's got."

"And Tom wants to walk. Don't you, Tom?"

Tom nodded.

Alistair sneered at such gross sucking-in. Then his attention was taken up by a shop window full of toys and novelties. He soon detected a doll that pee'd when it was filled with water. Permission to buy it was refused; he had known it would be and chuckled. Then he saw a tin full of stuff that made glorious bubbles when thrown from a ring. He had enough money to buy it.

"No," said his father, who then had a vision of thousands of iridescent bubbles floating into the sky above the hill. "All right. Hurry up."

While they were waiting for Alistair they saw Peerie again. About fifty yards along the street he peered from behind a pillar-box. Charlie fumed; it was really worse, he thought, than being out walking with a bitch in heat; in that case followers could be stoned.

When Alistair came out his purchase was at once confiscated.

"When we get to the top you'll get it," said his father.

They walked fast, to shake off Peerie; and with the same purpose they darted down two or three side streets, so that in the end Charlie himself was confused.

At length they came to the famous long flight of steps, where the road itself twisted like a serpent. At the bottom Charlie paused, to gaze up, and see ascending, nearly forty years ago, the diffident boy with the fat knees and the fist that was always clenched. "What's that you're gripping, Charles?" "Nothing, Mother." "A body would think it was a precious jewel." "No, Mother, it's nothing; look."

Looking now, he saw that his fist was indeed clenched; opened, it contained nothing still. He did not know whether to rejoice or grieve.

"I'll race you up," cried Alistair to the other two.

He raced up, but they waited for Forbes. It was not his son he saw on those steps; it was still that fat solemn boy who had seen the clouds at the top as castles in which giants lived, whom he must slay.

Slowly he began to climb. Halfway up, he had to rest, and take off his jacket.

"Look who's behind you, Dad!" yelled Alistair from the top.

He turned and saw Peerie at the foot.

"Go away," he cried, waving his hand. "Don't pester us."

A stranger glanced at him in surprise. Annoyed, he dashed up much too fast and arrived gasping.

"If we had a terrific boulder," said Alistair, "we could roll it down on top of him."

"Tom," called Peerie, in a forlorn voice.

"Go away," shouted Forbes. "Lead on, Alistair."

Past the lush fields they climbed, past the holiday camp with its châlets, and through the gate at last on to the golf course. Canada Hill was really the highest point of the course; crowned with pine trees, it was a popular and magnificent viewpoint.

On this green hill that boy with the chubby knees had been Balboa once. Today he was an unsuccessful dominie, still fat, still clutching nothing, but still surely with a trace of that wonder left. It was with a pang in his belly, though, that he heard Alistair shriek and saw him clamber up on to the cairn indicator, like an explorer claiming new territory. That enthusiasm could be shown only by those to whom the world was new, and whose explorations of their own beings still afforded joyful discoveries.

Near the cairn he raised his head, and was not disappointed. Arran towered, mauve and magnificent. The sky shone; below, glimpsed through the greenness of trees, stretched the Firth, a deeper blue, the shade of milkwort. The horizon was ringed with majestic clouds. A fragrant breeze blew. Somewhere, just the right distance away, in a Boys' Brigade camp beneath, a piper practised.

He sighed in gratitude: this loveliness then was not forfeit; indeed, now that his appreciation of it was scaled down to suit the quality and scope of his soul, his pleasure, expressed in this one sigh, was truer than last year's, when he had looked upon himself as a pilgrim at a shrine, and so had been goggle-eyed with ecstasy. That the restriction was just, and also humane, was proved by one glance at Tom now standing at the cairn, and by another at Peerie, the poor idiot in the coloured jockey cap, lurking behind a whin bush. As he made soberly for the cairn he realised that though he had not succeeded in saving Tom, he had at least been prevented from wrecking himself and the happiness of his family.

The grass around the cairn was littered with gluttonous sun-eaters, lying on their backs, with their mouths open. Young lovers lay entwined in public lust. Golfers searched leisurely for balls. Two ladies, like schoolmistresses on holiday, gently scolded Alistair for being on the indicator. A young father held his toddling daughter by the hand. An ugly woman showed too much thigh. Larks sang in the blue sky. Down the Firth, past the Isle of Cumbrae, sailed a large cargo boat, faithfully bound perhaps for some port on the other side of the world. Several pleasure steamers, from Dunroth, Wemyss Bay, Largs, and the Kyles of Bute, were making for Rothesay.

It was worth another sigh of gratitude.

"Well, Tom," he said, "isn't it fine?"

"Yes, sir."

The very meagreness of that response touched Charlie. How else expect the child from the hideous slum to respond to this abundance of beauty? Then he remembered that this cautious restraint might well be deliberate; behind it might lurk the thief, liar, betrayer, changeling. If it were so, it was occasion for grief, for silencing larks.

"What about my bubble stuff, Dad?" cried Alistair. "You said I'd get it at the top."

His father handed it over. "Let's go to the south cairn," he said. "We'll be able to see Towellan from there."

He led the way through the little pine wood. The path was overgrown with bramble bushes so that he had to thrust recklessly past in places. Hanging to one bush, like an obscene fruit, was an object, the most disenchanting on earth: a contraceptive. It was too high for him to kick it out of sight, and there was no time to search for a stick. He had to hurry past with a sudden shout to his followers to look at the hawk above them. It wasn't a hawk, only a gull. When he turned to examine their faces he could not tell whether his innocent lie had succeeded or not. Alistair was absorbed with his bubble apparatus; Gillian was as grave as a young nun; and Tom was as inscrutable as ever. As he stared at them, seeking signs of their having seen that dismal symbol here in the midst of nature's prodigality, he saw bobbing among the bushes another similar symbol, the red-blue-green-white cap of the halfwit pursuing them. He could not help connecting the one symbol with the other. Such as Peerie had no valid claim to existence.

Then, as he hastened on, the air about him began to glitter with bubbles, some small as marbles, some huge as footballs, and all rainbow-coloured. He snatched at them as they soared past. They were the pipe music grown visible. Their insubstantiality, and their dissolving so subtly into the sunshine, redeemed the grossness of his body, hot and sweaty and cleg-bitten, and the foolishness of his thoughts, so that for a few moments, for as long indeed as a bubble lasted, he felt wonderfully buoyant, a creature of light and faith and truth.

There were lovers by the south cairn, too, one pair in particular as rapt as nymph and satyr. Bubbles danced in profusion over them, and must have looked like true tributes from Venus. But Charlie, mindful of the duties of a twentieth-century parent, had to call to Alistair to be careful where he shed his bubbles. Not everyone would see the child as one of Venus's sprites, seated on the grass, and tossing with classic grace and magicality hundreds of bubbles into the air, as if he were giving the sunshine back to the sun.

Gillian was seated beside Alistair. Tom stood with him by the cairn. It was the opportunity Mary had advised him to seek.

He rested his arms on the cairn, and spoke in a quite neutral voice.

"Yonder's Towellan," he said, "up the coast from the lighthouse."

"Yes, sir."

"Well, Tom, you've been with us for a week now."

"Yes, sir."

"I think it's done you good physically. You're browner; you're a little heavier, I should say; you look healthier. Do you feel any better?"

This time there was hesitation, and then, most fleetingly, that smile about whose interpretation he and Todd had differed. Even now he found it hard to believe Todd was right.

"Yes, sir," said Tom at last.

"I wish we could have had you with us for a few days longer," said Forbes. "But it turns out now to be impossible, I'm afraid. You see, we got word this morning that a friend of Mrs Storrocks's is coming to stay with us for a few days. It's most unexpected, but — I'll let you into a secret, Tom — the cottage really belongs to Mrs Storrocks, so you'll understand we can't very well refuse. It means, you see, the hut will be required. However, the week you've had has likely had the best of the weather. The sun's shone every day, hasn't it? Yes, every single day."

"Where have I to go?"

The question astonished Forbes, especially as it didn't seem to be asked of him in particular; it was just breathed out to the air.

He had to answer it, however. "Home," he said, briskly. "Where we all end up sooner or later, home. Where else?"

"I cannae go there."

The sweat on Forbes had been cooling in the breeze; now at that anguished whisper it turned icy. He felt lost in a wilderness of thorned bushes to which clung contraceptives as numerous as Alistair's bubbles.

"I'm afraid, Tom," he muttered, "there's no help for it. I've explained why."

It was Gillian's turn to toss the bubbles; she did it with the grace of ballet. Amid the whins the lovers had become human again and discovered discretion; she smoothed down her dress, he tightened the knot in his tie.

Then Peerie began calling like a plaintive bird from among the pines. "Tom, Tom, I want to talk to you."

It might be as well, thought Forbes, if Tom was transferred to Brian Street as Todd and Mr Fisher had proposed.

"Where in God's name can you go," he asked, "if you don't go home?"

"I don't know."

Peerie kept calling.

Forbes grew angry. "There's no sense in taking up this attitude, Tom," he said. "You've had a good week out of it. That's always something. You'll go back looking the better for it. I know Mrs Forbes said last night you could stay for a few days more, but I've explained to you why that's now impossible. You'll be going tomorrow. I'll accompany you as far as Glasgow." He saw now he would be like an escort with a prisoner. "Donaldson's Court isn't a very pretty place, Tom, but it's your home. Your people live there."

Peerie called again.

"I wish to heaven you'd go and see what he wants," said Forbes. "I don't see what harm it can do. He's your friend, after all."

Tom shook his head.

The charge of heartlessness, made by Todd and others, must then be well founded. Because he was being sent home, for thieving and deceit as he well knew, he was showing this spite against his people and that poor fool in the cap. When I called him changeling, thought Forbes, I wasn't far wrong. How devilishly sly, really, to give his name to Mary over the telephone as "Tom Forbes". For the rest of their lives he, and perhaps Mary, too, would be haunted by this son never conceived and never born.

Peerie was still calling, monotonously and without hope.

"It's your business, Tom," said Forbes, "but I don't think it's right to harden your heart against your friends in this way."

Other cries were now disturbing the peace of the hilltop. Alistair was chasing Gillian, who had refused to give him back his bubble ring.

"That's enough," roared Forbes. "Give it to him."

Her obedience was so instant as to be almost insolent. She stopped and handed it over. Thereafter, she kept standing still, as if she was playing at Midas's daughter; the breeze, though, waved her hair. Then with mysterious devotion she began to walk through the trees to where Peerie called.

"Where do you think you're going?" shouted her father.

She pointed. "I thought if I went and talked to him, he'd be quiet."

"You'll do nothing of the kind. You've caused enough trouble."

The loudest cry of all was then heard. Throwing bubbles as he ran among the heather Alistair had fallen over a stone. He lay howling.

His father rushed towards him, but it was to the cairn that Gillian came.

"A traitor," she said to Tom, "is worse than a thief."

She thought, but couldn't be sure, so swiftly did he turn his face away and shut his eyes, that she had seen tears.

"Fifty thousand times worse," she added.

"For Christ's sake," he whispered, "leave me alane."

Assisted by his father, Alistair hirpled up to them. His knee bled. He tried bravely not to weep, but his snuffles of restraint were as loud as weeping.

"It's just a scratch," said his father, "nothing to make a fuss about."

Gillian looked at it. "No," she said.

"You keep quiet, Gillian," snapped her father. "His leg might have been broken for all the concern you showed."

"I'm sorry, Daddy. Shall I tie my hankie round it?"

Alistair nodded; if the blood was hidden, half the terror would go.

She put on the bandage with sarcastic tenderness.

"We'll have to take the bus down now, Dad," said Alistair, with gasps of regret.

"The sooner we're off this hill the better. I can't say I've enjoyed my visit, and it's the first time I haven't."

Alistair took an experimental step; he gasped and held on to the cairn. "You'll have to help me down to the bus, Dad."

"All right then, let's go."

Gillian was left at the cairn with Tom. "You wouldn't cry," she said, "if your leg was cut off, would you?"

This time, without any doubt, she did see tears. Laughing in triumph, to her father's indignation, she raced on ahead, down the green slope, through the gate, and into the bus.

There she sat, hands tranquilly on lap, and watched the others walk slowly where she had flown. Tom came last. His offer to help had not been accepted.

Gillian's lips moved, though she did not speak; the words they formed were: "For Christ's sake, leave me alane."

When he came into the bus she looked calmly to see if he had got rid of his tears; she was satisfied rather than disappointed when she saw he had. She paid no heed to her father's grumble that she had not helped. She felt in her mind at last easy, safe, and sure. It was all the greater shock, therefore, when, without any warning, or reason, her triumph vanished, like one of Alistair's bubbles, and in its place was a feeling of profoundest complicity with Tom. She knew now why he had stolen the tin-opener and ointment, and why he could not speak to Peerie.

When he sat down beside her and put his hands on his knees with a curious resoluteness, as if he was refusing to defend himself against her, it was her turn to feel tears in her eyes. All the way down to the pier she kept looking out of the window, wondering in what way she could help him.

CHAPTER
NINETEEN

On the steamer returning to Towellan Mary sat with her mother in the cosy saloon. Now that Tom knew he was to go home tomorrow, she thought it was time her mother was told, but she still wasn't sure whether she should be told the real reason.

It was Mrs Storrocks who brought up the subject of Tom.

"I'm not one who likes to admit she's wrong," she said, and grimly paused, "but I'm going to admit I was wrong about that boy."

Mary, who had been so right about Tom, at first didn't think of him. "What boy?"

"Tom. Tom Curdie. When you told me he was from a place like Donaldson's Court, I expected to find some freak that couldn't keep its nose clean, far less its mind. But that boy, given a chance, could take his place in any company."

Mary was fascinated by that grim charitableness, based on error.

"But I doubt if ever he'll get a chance. Charles says he's clever at his lessons?"

"Yes."

"I could believe it. You can hold an intelligent conversation with that boy."

Mary hadn't known such conversations between her mother and Tom had ever taken place. That he had listened, most respectfully, she was sure.

"And there's another thing I'll say in his favour: he never complains."

That was certainly true; and it sounded all the more creditable when said by one who herself complained often and proudly.

"I've never heard him grumble once!" said Mrs Storrocks, astounded. "Not once!"

No, thought Mary, he's much too sleekit for that.

"And it's not just that he's being polite with strangers. It's his nature not to grumble."

Mary was becoming uncomfortable.

"I wouldn't mind," said her mother, and paused to make a solemn mouth, "helping a boy like that. He's got brains and he's got natural good manners and he's got spunk. I hope Charles keeps an eye on him, and sees that he gets all the bursaries he's entitled to. And," here she again paused, to make an even more solemn mouth, "if there's ever anything I could do, within reason, I would be pleased to be consulted. I intend to have a serious talk with him before he goes back; that's to say, of course, if he keeps behaving as he's done up to now. Compare him with that oddity in the jockey's bonnet that's been following Charles about all afternoon: they're just not like two members of the same species."

Mary decided it was now time to speak. "I don't think you'll be having that serious talk with him, Mother."

"Why not? My money's my own, Mary. I can help whoever I like. Don't get alarmed. Gillian and Alistair are in a different category altogether; they're my own flesh and blood. Where he might get ha'pennies, they'll get pounds."

"I wasn't thinking of money at all," said Mary, considerably vexed. "It just so happens you're quite mistaken about him. He's taken you in just as he took Charlie in."

Mrs Storrocks laughed: the extravagance of that accusation of credulity rendered it without truth or insult.

"He's going home tomorrow," said Mary sharply.

"Tomorrow? As soon as that? I understood he was to be here another week, at least."

"So he was to be. He's being sent home."

"May I ask why? I've noticed things have been going on, mind you, that you and Charles have been keeping from me."

"We didn't want to spoil your holiday."

"That was considerate of you."

"He happens to be a thief; that's why he's being sent home."

Mrs Storrocks frowned. "A thief? That's a very serious thing to say."

"I know."

"Are you aware I've had occasion to compliment him on his honesty? Two or three times I've deliberately trusted him with my purse and handbag, and I've never lost so much as a ha'penny. What has he stolen?"

"Nothing in the house, so far as I know. He's too smart for that. When we were in Dunroth last Tuesday he lifted things from the counter in Woolworth's."

Mrs Storrocks was as indignant as if this attack was upon her own honesty; it was of course upon her judgment.

"Did you catch him at it? Has he confessed? Have you had a visit from the police, unknown to me?"

"Gillian saw him."

"Just Gillian?"

"Yes, just Gillian."

"There's no need to adopt that tone, Mary. It's the truth I'm after."

"I'm telling you the truth."

"It's one child's word against another child's."

"One of them happens to be your own grandchild."

"What did he say when you challenged him?"

"Nothing, because we didn't challenge him."

"You mean to say he's being sent home for stealing, and yet he's not been told it's for stealing?"

"That's right, Mother."

"Is this Charles's doing?"

"It's mine, too."

"I thought he was all for justice, especially for them who didn't normally get it? What was it Gillian saw him lift?"

Mary was silent: never had the nature of the theft seemed so absurd; and she wondered if she and Charlie hadn't really been too anxious to get rid of the boy.

"Well, Mary?"

"A tin-opener and a tin of ointment. Before you laugh, Mother, let me tell you this: that oddity in the jockey's bonnet, as you called him, admitted today, while he was talking to Gillian and Alistair, that he and Tom were members of a gang that lifted things from shops."

"That creature would admit he robbed the Bank of England if he thought you'd be interested. A tin-opener and a tin of ointment?"

"They're not so silly as you think. His friends are here camping; he was going to camp with them, after he left us; so a tin-opener would be useful."

"And the ointment?"

"Maybe he's got sores on his body somewhere."

"I've seen him almost naked, and there were no sores, Mary."

"Almost naked; there are places you haven't seen."

Mrs Storrocks was silent, save for two or three little reflective grunts. "What about the brooch? Did he steal that?"

"No, he bought it."

"I've been wondering why you weren't wearing it."

"Now you know."

"Stealing to me, Mary, is stealing, even if it's just a pin that's stolen. Make no mistake about that. I'd help a thief only as far as the jail. I wonder where he is?"

Mary was alarmed. "I'd rather you didn't say anything to him, Mother, especially here on the boat."

"You forget, Mary, it was me he deceived."

"He's deceived us all."

Her mother rose. "I'm just going to take a walk about the boat to stretch my legs."

"We're nearly at Towellan, Mother."

Mrs Storrocks looked out of the window. "We'll be five minutes yet. A lot of truth can be found out in five minutes."

Mary too had risen. "For heaven's sake, don't make a scene."

"There are times, Mary, when you seem to forget that I was in the world before you."

She found Tom standing in the coldest, and therefore the loneliest, part of the steamer, at the very front, on deck. She had to hold on to her hat as she approached him. To deceive anybody who had no business to be watching she put her hand on the boy's shoulder as she stooped and spoke into his ear.

"Is this true what I've just been told, that you lifted things from Woolworth's last Tuesday, without paying for them?"

His nod might have been a shiver of cold.

"A horse will nod," she said, "for it can't speak. You can speak. Did you steal?"

He spoke, and she heard, but it was not clear enough to satisfy her.

"I can hear the gulls," she said, "and the wind, but I can't hear you. Did you steal?"

"Yes."

She took her hand from his shoulder and rubbed it against her dress. "That's all I wanted to hear," she said, and went away.

She hadn't been his first visitor there in the bows. Gillian had been before her. She had come up silently and stood beside him for two or three minutes before speaking. Then she had just said: "I'm sorry, I'm terribly sorry." He had said nothing in reply, but had gone on biting at his fists on the rail. After another minute or two she had left, cold in body, but colder in mind. He seemed to her under some kind of doom, and though she felt she would have risked her life to help him his danger was such that no sacrifice on her part would be of any use.

When she was gone he had kept gnawing at his fists; but there was no way really by which the turmoil of despair within him could be stilled. Feeling his hands wet from his tears, he wished he could have been a crab at the dark bottom of the Firth. In his imagination he saw that crab entangled in strange submarine vegetation, and it was he.

CHAPTER
TWENTY

At Towellan Pier there was no bus to meet the steamer; there were a taxi and Willie's landau, but these were engaged.

Charlie was blamed.

"Now, Mrs Storrocks," he said reasonably, "you know we weren't sure what steamer we'd get back."

Though he didn't know it yet, he was really being blamed for Tom's deception of her.

"Well, go and see if the taxi will come back for us," said Mary.

"Can't we walk, my dear? It's a glorious evening."

"We've been walking all afternoon."

Making for a seat above the beach, Mary sat down. Her mother followed her.

Charlie passed Willie up on his perch, with whip ready. "I don't suppose you could come back for us, Willie?"

The old man shook his head. "Sorry, Mr Forbes," he said. "Sid Brown's just going a mile or so alang the road; he'll come back for you."

"Thanks, Willie." Though he knew he ought to be rushing over to catch Brown before he left, Charlie wasted seconds in patting the horses.

Willie grinned down at him oddly. "I see you've got visitors," he said.

"Visitors?" Charlie glanced round.

"At the cottage. Weel, I take it they're visitors. They were making themselves at hame on your front lawn as I passed by."

"Did they have a tent?"

Willie laughed. "I didnae notice it, but I wouldnae be surprised."

"Why?"

But Willie was away, with his horses trotting smartly, and his passengers looking down like usurpers.

Sid Brown was willing to come back; he promised not to be long.

Charlie strolled over to his family.

"Just five minutes, to wait," he said, "and the finest of sunshine to wait in."

"And the biggest midges to bite us," said Mary.

Scratching himself, he noticed Tom Curdie down on the beach, seated on a rock. Such public segregation struck him as indiscreet, unnecessary, and vindictive.

"Was it the midges drove Tom down to the beach?" he asked.

"Likely enough," said Mary.

"No," remarked her mother coolly, "it was me. I let him understand I had no wish to associate with thieves."

"Mother!"

Charlie gazed in impotent anger from his wife to his mother-in-law.

"Yes, Charles," said the latter, "I'm in the secret; so it's not a secret any longer; and it should not be a secret."

"Who's a thief?" asked Alistair.

"You see, Mother, what you've started," said Mary.

"I have started nothing, Mary; in fact, I've ended something. The thief, Alistair, is that boy down on the beach."

There were several boys on the beach.

"The one sitting on the rock there, with his chin on his hands."

"But that's Tom, Grannie."

"So it is."

"But what did he steal?"

"For one thing," said his grandmother sternly, "he stole my trust; and I'll tell you this, if you steal my trust you'll be like the dirt under my feet for as long as you live."

That speech, which displeased Mary and horrified Charlie, also mystified Alistair into temporarily losing interest in Tom the thief.

"It may interest you all to know," said Charlie, with a bitterness not belonging to his words, "that we have visitors."

Mary glanced round and saw only some gulls on a dyke.

"I mean, at the cottage, waiting for us. So Willie told me."

"Was it that old fool?" asked Mrs Storrocks in scorn. "His wits are wandered. It comes of talking too much to his horses."

"I hope to heaven he was havering," said Mary. "I'm in no mood for visitors." Suddenly she put her hand to her mouth in horror. "Don't tell me they're Tom's pals?"

"No. Willie said they had no tent."

"They wouldn't be carrying it about with them, would they? Surely he said who they were? I mean, are they adults or children."

"He didn't say."

"But didn't you ask him?"

"I hadn't time."

"You had time to clap the horses, Charles," said Mrs Storrocks. "It might be Bess McCormick and her husband, very good friends of mine. I believe they're in a hotel at Hunter's Quay this fortnight. He's very keen on yachting. Did that old fool say if there was a car at the gate? They've got a new one, that cost well over a thousand pounds."

"He said nothing about a car," replied Charlie, wondering if Willie's peculiar grin might be explained by the gleaming opulence of the car at the gate. Willie had a contempt for cars and their owners.

"If it is Bess and Ronald," said Mrs Storrocks, "I'd be obliged if a certain somebody's kept safely locked away until they go away."

"He's not a leper," protested Charlie.

"He's worse; he's a thief."

"Well," said Mary, rising, "we'll soon find out, for here's the taxi."

Tom Curdie offered to walk.

"Why not?" said Mrs Storrocks. "Apart from anything else, it's ridiculous that a boy of your age should be carried about in taxis."

"I'll walk, too," said Gillian.

"Nobody will walk," said her mother. "There's room for us all."

They climbed in. Alistair sat on his father's knee, huffed because he had wanted to sit beside the driver; that place of honour had been given to Tom. It was, Alistair thought and even muttered, an act of theft. Thus was his grandmother's seed germinating. His father breathed violent threats into his ear.

The journey took four minutes. As they drew up at the gate the driver grinned at Tom. From behind came shocked noises. Jumping down, he opened the door. "I see you've got visitors," he said.

"For God's sake," muttered Charlie, trying to smile, "they're no visitors of ours."

"They'll be tinks in cadging."

"Yes, that's who they'll be."

Consternation rather than generosity made the tip large.

There were four of them. One was a bloated woman in a mauve coat, almost the same shade as Charlie's shorts; it was long in tinker fashion, down to the ankles to save the trouble of clean legs. Those legs were covered in loose, laddered, and holey nylons. Where one of the coat buttons was missing a large brass safety-pin took its place. She wore no hat, and her hair, long and lank and rusty with dyes, was arranged in an attempt at fashion and glamour. Since she had teeth missing her leer of welcome seemed menacing and half-witted. Beside her, clinging to her indeed, was a man as small as a dwarf, but at least twenty years her senior. His legs were deformed, so that walking, so simple for chickens even, was for him a heroic labour, harrowing to watch. Perhaps because of his struggles to move from one spot to another no better, his small grey face was almost malevolent. In his hand he held a cap; it looked as frightening as a cudgel as it swung in his contortions.

The two others were children, one a boy smaller than Alistair, with his face blemished by about a dozen sores, all painted with a violet antiseptic; the other a fair-haired toddler of about three, in whose hand was a bunch of flowers evidently plucked from the garden.

"This is a case for the police," said Mrs Storrocks.

"A shilling will get rid of them," muttered Charlie.

"Then go and give it to them, for heaven's sake," whispered Mary.

Led by him, they advanced through the gate.

The little girl was released by her mother, like a puppy, and came staggering towards them, with inarticulate shrieks.

"She's filthy," hissed Mrs Storrocks, "and she stinks."

Even the fragrance of the flowers could not subdue that smell.

"And she could be quite a bonny little thing," said Mary.

Then the child was among them. They drew back, so that she went straight to Tom, offering him the flowers. To their amazement, instead of pushing her away as

226

they would have done, he held his hand above her head as if he wished to pat her but could not. His hand shook.

They realised the shrill noises she was making were his name.

"She's Molly," he said, "my half-sister."

"And those?" whispered Charlie, indicating the trio now upon them.

Tom nodded; his face twitched; his eyes, wishing desperately to achieve their old impassiveness, could not.

Compassionate amusement should have been the reaction, but Charlie couldn't manage it. On the contrary, he found himself slipping into a panic of anger at these ridiculous intruders, and at this boy who was responsible for bringing them here. When he glanced at his wife's face he saw that she too was missing the fun of this contretemps.

His mother-in-law gaped like a gargoyle of disgust.

Mrs Curdie, on the contrary, cackled good-naturedly at their astonishment. The stench of beer and whisky from her did not quite overwhelm a whiff of insanitariness.

"I can see ye're a' surprised to see us," she cried happily. "We're no' ones for writing aheid to warn folk. I hope ye'll pardon us the liberty o' making oorsel's at hame." She laughed so much she slavered, and wiped it off on her sleeve. "We're no' exactly strangers, ye ken. I kent it was you, Mr Forbes, as soon as ye stepped oot the caur, for I once had ye pointed oot to me in the street near the school. I'll no' say whit name was attached to ye then, for we a' ken whit like weans are wi' teachers' names." After a shriek of mirth, she turned to Mary. "If ye'll no' think me awfu' cheeky for saying it, Mrs Forbes, ye're looking the picture o' health. Aye, and your weans too. I was just saying that to Shoogle here — Mr Kemp, I should say: he's Tom's uncle, ye ken. Aye." She laughed in happy derision at her own lie. "But I'm no' being mannerly. I should be introducing ye properly to my ain family. This is Alec — ye're no' to be feart o' the scabs, the doctor assured us they're no' smittal. And this is Molly, oor wee pet. I hope ye don't mind us picking a wee bunch o' your braw flowers for her? Christ's truth, it was either that or haeing her demolish the whole gairden. And o' coorse there's nae need for me to introduce my clever boy Tom. I hope he's been behaving himself. Hae you, Tommy?" But she took care not to let her doting leer dwell on him too long.

The little man, even at rest precariously and painfully balanced, tried not to look undignified, and succeeded only in looking sly, mean, and querulous. He too stank of alcohol.

"It was sich a fine day," he whined, "we thought we'd pay Tom a visit."

"That's right," yelped Mrs Curdie. "Being a mither yoursel', Mrs Forbes, ye'll understaun' that I've been anxious aboot my boy, my son and heir, as you might say. Oh hell, I kent you would be looking after him weel, but a mither's never at rest in her he'rt till she's seen for hersel'."

Charlie was thinking, "What can I say, what am I to do, how do I get rid of them?"

It was Mary who took charge.

"Yes, I understand, Mrs Curdie," she said. "But we can't stand here and be eaten by the midges."

Mrs Curdie shrieked at that jest. "Aren't they the wee buggers, hen?" And she clawed at herself vigorously.

Mary led the way up to the house. "You'll be feeling like a cup of tea before you go for your steamer?"

Mrs Curdie winked at the sky; for only it could have withstood the effrontery of such a wink.

"To tell you the Christ's truth, hen," she whispered, "we were hoping you could squeeze us in for the night. You can see for yoursel' that wee Molly's fair tired oot, and it wad be a shame dragging her a' the way back to Glesca withoot a night's rest. And Alec here, poor wee fellow, 's been craving a' week to see his brither."

Mary was almost shamed into a silence that would have meant consent; just in time, roused by her mother's nudge and snort, she cried: "Oh, I'm afraid that's impossible, Mrs Curdie. We haven't got nearly enough room."

Mrs Curdie shook her head sportively, as if to say that though the lie was well told, it could hardly deceive so expert a liar as herself.

"Ugh, it's a mansion, hen," she said, with a sly keek at the house.

"I'm afraid it's far from that. It's got only three bedrooms."

Mrs Curdie counted the whole company; she kept cackling at the easiness of their disposal, if it was left to her.

Shoogle tugged her. "The hut, Queenie," he whispered.

She nodded, as if she had that trump well in mind. "There's a braw hut at the back, hen," she said, "that wad dae us fine. We took the liberty o' peeping in the window. There's a bed in it. That's a' we need, just a bed."

"I'm afraid that's where Tom sleeps."

Mrs Curdie brooded. "So he's no' in the house wi' the rest o' ye?"

"No. There wasn't room."

Mrs Curdie nodded, with a sad sneer at that inevitable inhumanity.

"I assure you it's very comfortable," said Mary, who then turned upon her husband and with outraged eyes demanded that he stop grinning like a gomeril and help her to get rid of this bloodsucking witch from slumdom.

He was grinning so foolishly because it had occurred to him that here was the opportunity for a grand Samaritan gesture: take in these wretched specimens of humanity, feed them, cherish them, sleep them in comfortable beds, while he and his family slept on chairs or floor. Todd, Mr Fisher, and all the rest, would no doubt be smugly amused when they heard that he had been forced to send Tom home after a week, but that amusement would die of excess, when they learned of this prodigious hospitality. But it could not be. What had been proved on Canada Hill, amidst the beauty and grandeur there, was proved again here, in the presence of this unwholesome human rubbish: his heart was of ordinary size, composition, and quality; only if he acted accordingly would he find peace; that it would be the peace of mediocrity could not be helped.

Therefore he faced up to Mrs Curdie and told her what countless millions would.

"I'm afraid, Mrs Curdie," he said, "that what my wife says is the case. We'd like to put you up, but it's just not possible. What we will do, though, after you've had some tea, is to see that you get safely on the bus that gets into Dunroth in time for the last steamer. That bus will pass here in under an hour, so we've no time to waste."

She ogled him. "If it was just Shoogle and me," she coaxed, "we wouldnae mind; but we hae these poor wee souls to consider."

"Did you consider them when you came here uninvited, at such a late hour, after spending on drink what could have bought you hotel accommodation?"

That pertinent and comprehensive question was put by Mrs Storrocks.

"Ye're misunderstaun'in us," whined Mrs Curdie. "We met some freens in Dunroth. They would hae us in for a drink, just to celebrate meeting them, ye ken. We spent no' a ha'penny. May I drap deid this very minute, here at your very doorstep, if I'm telling a lee."

She seemed to wait, with a glance upward and some anxiety. Shoogle too was anxious. When the moment was past, he said, belching boldly, "We hae nae money to spend on drink."

"Maybe you don't think it's wasted, of course," said Mrs Storrocks, as she marched into the house.

Mary hesitated on the threshold. "Perhaps you'd rather stay out in the sunshine till the tea's ready?"

Mrs Curdie came closer. "Ye're forgetting the midges, hen. They've got wee Molly in lumps. And to tell you the truth, as woman to woman, there's a place I'm bursting to visit. The rest o' them went up into the wood at the back o' your hoose, but that's a thing I just cannae bring myself to dae: it's no' ladylike oot o' doors. Eh?"

They entered. Mary flung open the door of the sitting-room and cried to Tom, although she couldn't see him, "Tom, will you take your friends in here, and make them comfortable until tea's ready?"

Mrs Curdie whispered, "I'll never be comfortable, hen, till ye've opened anither door, wi' a sicht o' wally."

"Come with me," said Mary. As she ran upstairs she was wondering how she could have the seat disinfected before anybody else used it. "Here you are," she said.

Mrs Curdie looked in. "It's braw," she said, with a sigh. "A body could sit in there wi' pleasure. Ye should see the place we hae at hame, hen."

Mary did not wait to hear about the place at home. In her bedroom she stood before the mirror, with her hands squeezing her face into a mask of horror. Yet she could not keep humour out, and the noise in the room was her own laughter. "Poor Charlie," she kept saying, "poor Charlie." The pity was affectionate. If anything

232

else had been needed to prove to him that his bringing of Tom had been a blunder, here it certainly was; and it proved it to her, too. As a consequence she hurried downstairs, able to do what was necessary.

In the dining-room she found Charlie, Alistair, and Gillian huddled together at the window.

"Where's my mother?" she asked.

"In the sitting-room."

"With them?"

"Yes. She said somebody ought to go in and see nothing was damaged or stolen. She thought it was my duty. Mine!"

He was astonished and then huffed by his wife's laughter.

"Cheer up, Charlie," she cried. "It won't last for ever. Help me to get the tea ready. What were you looking at out there?"

"Tom," replied Alistair. "He won't come in."

"You be quiet," whispered his sister.

Mary glanced out.

"He's hiding behind the tree, Mummy," said Alistair.

"Why? What's the matter with him?"

"I know," said Gillian.

"Do you, Gillian?"

"Your mother," said Charlie to the children, "has apparently seen the humour of the situation."

"And thank heaven I have," cried Mary, "otherwise I'd be weeping." Again she laughed, and felt like taking Charlie's hands and dancing a step or two with him. The next half hour would be weird and awful, but at the end of it all the visitors, Tom included, would have gone. Then the holiday would begin, and the fun of this evening would be remembered for years.

"Hurry up," she cried. "We can't have them missing that bus. You put on the kettle, Charlie. Gillian, you set the table."

"How many places will I set?"

"Oh, yes, there's that, isn't there? We don't want to have tea with them, do we?"

Alistair shuddered. "No. That boy's face, it's all blue scabs!"

"He can't help that," said Gillian sharply.

"It would make me sick."

"You're a silly little snob. Do you think your own table manners are perfect?"

"If it's a bad prune," he said indignantly, "do you want me to swallow it and die?"

Aware of the imperfections of her own family, Mary was exhilarated rather than depressed; she loved them all the more. In the kitchen when Charlie, cutting bread, turned to smirk reproach, she laughed so much she had to hold on to him.

"Are you sure you're not a trifle hysterical, my dear?" he asked.

"I'm sure I am," she replied. "But, oh, Charlie, did you ever see such a creature in all your life?"

"Which one?" His voice was cold and sad.

"The woman!"

"I must warn you, Mary, that if they hear you laughing like that they'll be encouraged, and will be as hard to shift as limpets."

234

"Och, limpets are easy," said Alistair. "All you need to do is to give them a sudden kick."

"That's it," cried his mother. "We'll give them tea, and then a sudden kick. They'll be in the bus before they know it."

"These limpets are cunning," warned Charlie.

Gillian looked into the kitchen. "What about Tom?" she asked.

Her mother smiled. "Well, what about him?"

"Is he to have tea with them, or with us?"

"With them, of course. As a matter of fact, Charlie, I think it would be a good idea if he went home with them."

Reluctantly he nodded.

"So will you go and tell him to get packed?"

"Me?"

"Yes, Charlie, you. You brought him."

"I'll never be forgiven that," he cried. "I'm busy here. There's Gillian, she can go and tell him."

"She certainly won't. Is he still out in the garden?"

"Yes, Mummy," said Gillian.

"You'd think, after what's happened here, he'd be glad to see his people. To us she's hideous, but to him she's his mother."

"I doubt," said Charlie, "if she's half as hideous to us as she is to him."

"Charlie, that's a terrible thing to say!"

"Is there anything else you want me to do?" asked Gillian.

"Yes," said her mother. "I'd like you to take Alistair out of the way till these people have gone."

"I want to stay," protested Alistair. "I've got a sore leg."

"You could go and lie down on your bed for half an hour."

"I want to stay."

"Let him stay," said his father bitterly. "The experience will be educative."

"May I go myself?" asked Gillian.

"Of course, if you want to," said her mother. "Is there anything wrong?"

"No, Mummy." What was wrong really was that she felt for the boy hiding behind the tree an understanding and pity, neither of which could be expressed; but it did not seem worthwhile to say so; to anybody, especially to her parents.

In the hall Gillian met Mrs Curdie admiring the grandfather clock. She had washed her hands with scented soap and sprinkled perfumed talcum powder over her face.

"Whit's your name, hen?" she asked.

"Gillian."

"That's a nice name, and I can see you're a nice lassie. I'm sure you and my Tom hae got on weel."

Mrs Forbes came into the hall. "Oh, there you are, Mrs Curdie," she said. "Tea's ready. Gillian, will you go and tell Tom?"

"Where is he?" asked his mother.

"Out in the garden."

Mrs Curdie sighed loudly. "He never was one for staying in the hoose much," she said. "But I thought it would be different wi' such a braw hoose as this. To tell you the Christ's truth, hen, he's my ain son, but I hae never understood him. There are times when he makes me feel I'd get mair consideration frae him if I was a beetle he had accidentally tramped on. For he's no' a hard-hearted boy: he's got kind words for stray cats, but nane for his mither. Would it be his brains, d'you think? It's no' guid for ye haeing mair than ye can cope wi'."

Mary felt moved; at the same time she wished Gillian hadn't heard. "I understand, Mrs Curdie," she murmured. "I suppose it is a difficult position. Perhaps you'd like to go yourself and fetch him in? I'll tell the others."

Hurrying into the sitting-room, as a refuge from that pudgy, forlorn, silly face, she found Kemp and the boy seated side by side on the sofa, with her mother as vigilant and relentless as a jailer. At her feet, on newspapers, sat the little girl, sleepily holding the flowers.

Despite the flowers, it was immediately obvious why Molly was seated on newspapers: it was to protect the carpet; she stank worse than ever. The jailer's resoluteness was all the more praiseworthy.

"Tea's ready," announced Mary. "The guests are having theirs first, Mother. They've got that bus to catch."

"I've been keeping my eye on the clock, Mary. This child will have to be changed."

"Yes."

"They have no change with them."

"But she can't travel like that."

"It seems she can, and does, frequently."

"Perhaps I can find an old towel that would do." Mary made to pick up the infant.

The little man wriggled off the sofa. "Leave her to me, Mrs Forbes," he said.

"Are you sure?"

"I dae it often. Ther's naething I like better."

He picked up his daughter tenderly.

"I doubt if it's safe," said Mrs Storrocks bluntly. "In the first place, are you sober enough?"

"I would never fa' wi' wee Molly in my airms," he said, with passion. "Would I, pet? Even if a bus was to run into me, I wouldnae let you drap."

Mrs Storrocks was shocked by that fiasco of affection.

"Maybe you'd better change her in the bathroom," said Mary. "It's upstairs, though."

"I can climb stairs, lady. I earn my living."

"And I'm going out for some fresh air," said Mrs Storrocks.

Mary was left with the boy with the violet scabs. She began to think that she might not after all get rid of her guests that night. If she didn't, she would become ill-tempered enough to satisfy even Charlie.

CHAPTER
TWENTY-ONE

Standing on the steps at the front of the house, Mrs Storrocks saw Mrs Curdie talking to Tom under the beech tree. Gillian stood beside them, near enough for contamination.

"Gillian!" she shouted.

Gillian turned, saw her grandmother's peremptory wave, and slowly came over, pale and trembling.

"What's wrong?" demanded her grandmother. "Have those riffraff been pestering you? Hadn't you the sense to keep back from them?"

Gillian shook her head; if she had tried to speak, she would have wept; and both speech and tears would have been unintelligible to her grandmother.

Going out to Tom, Mrs Curdie had needed support; she had sought it from Gillian, seizing the girl's hand in hers, and dragging her towards Tom. As soon as his mother had begun to speak, in a whining tone of entreaty, he had with his right fist struck the tree several times, deliberately, with all his force, so that his mother had shrieked and blood had spurted from his knuckles, staining the trunk. His mother had tried to stop him, to catch his hand and kiss it, but he had repulsed her, almost knocking her over. She had even offered her own face, no more percipient than the tree, but softer, for him to punch. He had stopped then, and his hand by his side had dripped blood on to the grass.

"What are they plotting?" asked Mrs Storrocks.

Again Gillian shook her head.

"Don't let them upset you, Gillian. Towards scruff of that sort make your heart like a stone. Keep your sympathy for those who'll appreciate it. I hope your father has realised that that boy's to go home with the rest of them tonight. No, it won't have occurred to him. You and I, Gillian, are the ones who keep our eyes open. Go in and tell your father; or better still, your mother. It'll not take two minutes to pack his case."

Gillian did not move.

"Gillian, I asked you to go and tell your mother."

"I'm sorry, Grandma, I can't." And still not weeping, Gillian ran away, round to the back of the house.

Her grandmother angrily breathed in the scent of roses and tang of seaweed. She could not remember having seen Gillian get a good old-fashioned thrashing. The result was this thrawn disobedient girl with too much wilful nonsense in her head.

Mrs Curdie and Tom were coming across the lawn towards the house. They did not walk hand-in-hand, like mother and son; she cringed, as if asking a favour from someone far above her in station; and truly his face was hard and aloof, like a young prince's out of a story-book. By his side his hand hung, bright with blood.

When she reached Mrs Storrocks, Mrs Curdie gazed up no higher than the gold locket round the pink plump neck.

240

"There's sich a thing," she snuffled miserably, "as being too clever for your ain guid. Whit it is that's broken his he'rt, I cannae say. Maybe ye'd think it was haeing me for his mither, and poor Shoogle for his faither. But it's no that, either, for he's never complained aboot us. You expect a wean to be greedy; but never him. Whit there was for eating, he ate; whit there was for wearing, he wore; whit was missing, he did withoot; and never once did he complain. But a' the time his he'rt's been breaking."

Mrs Storrocks was astonished and displeased: she had not credited this hag with such eloquent sorrow; and the discovery warned her there might be more. It was not the first time she had found to her indignation that people were more valuable than she had thought, or indeed than they deserved to be.

The boy, too, wore that look of superiority. In his case it was impertinence to the point of lunacy. Was he not a thief, and had he not been cradled in rags and filth and poverty?

Yet his hand red with blood was like an emblem of eerie distinction.

"What's the matter with his hand?" she asked.

"He banged it against the tree."

"Why? Has he gone crazy?"

Then they were joined by Mary who came out, cheerfully, to tell them tea was waiting, and the bus was due in twenty-five minutes.

"He'll have to go and wash his hand first," said her mother.

"We've no time to spare for that, Mother."

"Look at it."

He had put it behind his back.

"Show your hand to Mrs Forbes," said Mrs Storrocks sternly.

"Let me see it, Tom?" asked Mary.

Slowly he showed it. So lacerated and bloody, it made her cry out.

"How on earth —?"

"He banged it, if you please, against the tree," said her mother.

"Why?"

"Spite, if you ask me; spite and temper."

Mary shook her head: that explanation, which put all the blame on the child, was much too simple.

Charlie came out, determined to be cheerful. He noticed that the Firth was a strange lovely pink colour, and it gave him courage.

"You'll have to hurry, Mrs Curdie," he cried, "or that little boy of yours will have cleared all the plates."

"He'd eat soap," she admitted.

"Look at his hand, Charlie," whispered Mary.

When he saw it he glanced in alarm towards the sea. "My God, how did this happen?" he cried.

"Never mind that now," said Mary. "It'll have to be washed and disinfected. Will you take him upstairs and do it, Charlie? It's making me feel sick. It must be terribly painful. He may have to see a doctor. They'll never catch that bus tonight, I can see that."

As he set out disinfectant, cottonwool, bandages, scissors, and adhesive, Charlie's hands were clumsy with nervousness and guilt. He had already suspected

242

that by bringing Tom to Towellan he had, inexplicably, done the boy more harm than good; now this self-inflicted injury was no doubt the outward sign of that harm. But what dreadful spiritual stress had been responsible he did not know, and did not really want to know. Such knowledge he had not the imagination to acquire, nor the courage and compassion to bear.

He tried to speak cheerfully. "If it'd been Alistair who'd got a hand like this," he said, "he'd have made a row that could be heard across in Rothesay." But even as he uttered that disloyalty his heart was warm with love for his son, whose howling and fuss would have been a clamour for help and sympathy, so much preferable to this inhuman silence and endurance.

Yet for his own sake he hoped that silence would not be broken. If Tom pleaded, if he wept in pain or penitence or unhappiness, he might weep too, at his own futility.

The wound was washed with tenderness, disinfected, smeared with soothing ointment, and now was ready for the bandage. The long white strip of cloth reminded Charlie of the cerements of a mummy; and somehow the resemblance did not seem so fantastic when he glanced aside at that small remote indecipherable face.

"I stole Mr Todd's money," said Tom.

Charlie stopped bandaging. The very sound of the words had disconcerted him too much to grasp their meaning.

"What's that, Tom?"

"I stole Mr Todd's money."

Charlie tried to laugh. "Don't take everything on yourself, boy," he said.

"I took it. I broke into the school."

"But you denied it so confidently when Mr Todd and Mr Fisher questioned you!"

Tom smiled: it was the same swift smile with which he had entered Mr Fisher's room to undergo that questioning. Was it then, after all, a smile of subtlest insolence, of changeling malice?

"I don't believe it, Tom," said Charlie. "You're just piling blame on yourself because you're unhappy."

"And I took the half-crowns out of your desk."

Only Charlie and the thief knew those half-crowns had been stolen.

"How many were there?" asked Charlie hoarsely.

"Six."

"Yes, six." Charlie too smiled, in anguish. With what confidence had he undertaken a task so immeasurably beyond his powers! Into what wild dark realms of tragedy had he walked, with his few matches of faith? Instead of Todd's sarcasm and the amused pity of the others, should have been the roaring of the incensed gods.

There was an imperative rattling at the door handle, as if, indeed, the messenger at last had come, to summon for retribution; but when the door opened it was Alistair who peeped in.

"Mum says you've to go down as quick as you can," he said.

"Yes, all right. I've just finished."

Alistair glanced at the bandage, and then at the strip of Elastoplast on his own knee. He sneered, indicating his opinion that the smaller the covering the greater the courage.

"Tom's to go, too," he added.

Charlie hurried down, leaving Tom to linger on the stairs.

When he entered the dining-room he saw at once something serious was amiss. Never had he seen Mary look so disgusted. Her mother stood in the doorway leading to the kitchen, looking outraged, but enjoying it.

The boy with the scabs was still eating; the little girl was asleep, with a jammy piece of bread at her mouth. The cripple nibbled at a cake, like a cannibal at a piece of rancid flesh. Mrs Curdie was munching and talking.

"Nae wean breaks his haun against a tree for nothing," she was saying. When she saw Charlie, she cried: "Where's my Tommy? Whit hae you done wi' him?"

"As you know, Mrs Curdie, I've been bandaging his hand."

"Charles," said his mother-in-law, "I think you should be warned that a very nasty insinuation has been made about you. For your own protection I think you should go right out to the hall and telephone for the police."

He looked in amazement at Mary. She nodded. "I'm afraid so, Charlie," she said. "Read this." She snatched up a scrap of paper from the floor and handed it to him, with as much revulsion as if it was smeared with excrement.

"That was tore frae the paper just last Sunday," said Mrs Curdie.

It was about a schoolmaster found guilty of sexual offences against boys under his care.

"You'll see he got eighteen months," said Mrs Curdie, "and of coorse his career's ruined."

"Where did this come from?" asked Charlie.

"They brought it," said Mary.

"I'm no' blaming you, hen," whined Mrs Curdie.

"Are you blaming me?" shouted Charlie.

"No' exactly blaming you, Mr Forbes. But, ye see, these things happen, and a mither's got to be carefu'. Then when ye were sae anxious to get rid o' us, it looked suspeecious. And poor wee Tommy, he's sae terrible upset aboot something."

"No damned wonder he's upset," roared Charlie. "Will I tell you why? He's upset because he's a rotten little lying thief, and he's been found out."

"A thief!" wailed Mrs Curdie. "Oh my God, Shoogle, did you hear that? He ca'ed Tommy a thief."

"I've listened to enough," said Mrs Storrocks, marching to the door. "If you're not out of here in five minutes, taking your precious son with you, I shall phone for the police. Where is he, Charles?"

"He came down the stairs behind me. Maybe he's gone outside."

"Daddy, Daddy!" It was Alistair shouting, and in he raced, gasping with excitement. "Police. The police are coming."

Mrs Curdie leered at him. "You're weel-trained, son," she said, "but ye'll hae to do better than that to take in Queenie Curdie."

Mary looked out of the window. A large car was stopped at the gate. Two policemen stood beside it, and were apparently about to come up to the house.

"They're at the gate all right," she said.

She and Charlie hurried to the outside door.

"Do you think it's the Woolworth's business?" she whispered.

"No. How can it be? It'll be some routine inquiry."

"About what?"

"I don't know."

They were joined by Mrs Curdie. "Shoogle and me hae agreed," she said, sniggering anxiously, "that we'll let the maitter drap. The less we hae to dae with these bastards the better." She hurried back into the house.

There was a sergeant and a constable.

"Mr Forbes?" asked the sergeant.

"That's me," said Charlie. "And this is my wife."

The sergeant touched his helmet. "I'm Sergeant McBrayne, and this is Constable Rankin. We're sorry to trouble you. You're on holiday here?"

"Yes. This is my wife's cousin's house, Mrs McDaid."

"That's right. Have you a boy called Curdie living with you?"

"So it is him," said Mary.

The sergeant stared at her. "Aye, Mrs Forbes, it is."

"Perhaps you'd better step inside, Sergeant," said Charlie.

"Well, if you don't mind. The midges are bad."

As they went into the sitting-room the sergeant saw Alistair in the hall. "This isn't him?"

"No, that's our son Alistair," said Mary.

"Sorry, Mrs Forbes. I should have known. Curdie's a bit older, isn't he? Where is he?"

"At the back somewhere," said Charlie. "Do you want to see him?"

"It's what we're here for."

Charlie sent Alistair, who raced off, smacking his hip.

In the sitting-room they sat down, the policemen with their helmets on their knees. Mary sat on the arm of Charlie's chair.

"Just to get things right, Mr Forbes," said the sergeant, "I wonder if you'd explain your connection with Curdie."

"That's easily done. I'm his teacher. He comes from a slum, and his people are pretty horrible. They're in the house at the moment pestering us. I was sorry for him, so I brought him here for a holiday with my family."

"I see. Hasn't it turned out as well as you'd expected? I mean, you sound a shade disappointed, if you'll pardon me saying so."

"It hasn't turned out well at all," said Mary.

"Might I ask why?"

It was Charlie who answered. "I'm afraid we've found him sly, secretive, and deceitful, and not the kind of companion we like for our own children."

"I see. Have you missed anything? I mean, have you reason to believe he's stolen anything?"

248

"No."

"You'd be on the look-out for that, of course. Being his teacher, you'd know he was on probation?"

"Yes, I knew that."

"Aye. So his folk are here? That's handy."

"Not for us," said Charlie grimly. "We've been trying to get rid of them."

The sergeant laughed. "What's keeping him, though? I think you'd better take a look, Geordie."

The policeman got up and went out.

"What's he done, Sergeant, that brings you here?" asked Charlie. "We've had him under strict supervision."

"Have you heard of Chick Mackie and Peerie Whitehouse?"

"Vaguely."

"Well, we've got them in the car at the gate. They're friends of Curdie's, I understand."

"I believe so."

"This boy Mackie, he stole a handbag this morning in Dunroth. The silly woman left it lying on the seat beside her, turned her head for a second, and it was gone; and the forty-five pounds that were in it."

"Forty-five pounds!" cried Mary and Charlie together.

"Aye, and we haven't got it back yet. Mackie seems something of an imbecile, but he knows how to hold his tongue."

"Tom was in Towellan all morning," said Mary.

"That's right. We know Mackie did it on his own, but it seems Curdie's the master-mind behind the scenes."

"It doesn't need much of a master-mind," said Charlie, "to plan a snatch from a seat in broad daylight."

"No, that's right."

Then in raced Alistair again. "Daddy! Mummy!" he gasped.

"What is it?" they cried.

"It's Tom. He's run away. He's disappeared."

The sergeant jumped to his feet. "If you'll excuse me," he said, and hurried out.

Alistair looked at his parents, as if he had them at his mercy. "And Gillian's gone with him," he suddenly shouted.

CHAPTER
TWENTY-TWO

The truth was, Tom had gone with Gillian. Seeing the police she had rushed to the hut where he was seated on the bed, with his case open at his feet.

"Hurry," she cried, "hurry."

He thought she meant the bus would be along soon; her agitation of tears was caused by joy at his leaving. But he had not been able to face the prospect of returning with his mother and Alec and Molly, and so he shook his head.

"Yes, you must come," she cried. "You can't just sit there and let them catch you."

Taking him by the unbandaged hand she pulled him out of the hut, down the garden, and through the gate leading into the wood.

He thought her intention after all must be to help him, to hide him somewhere until the bus, with the others in it, was gone. So he went willingly, running after her through the shadowy wood, over the steep field in which the whins lay like golden cattle, and beyond the drystone dyke up the hillside where the bracken was thick and higher than their heads.

"We'll go to the shepherd's hut," she gasped. "It's up the hill a good bit, in a hollow. It's where the shepherd stays at lambing-time. If we creep through the bracken to the burn we'll be able to get up without being seen. I'll go first and make a way. You've only got one hand."

Though she still shed tears, and spoke through sobs, there was now a brightness about her, like sunshine through rain. The glances she kept casting back were far more defiant than his, and the eagerness with which she burrowed through the tunnel of bracken was in contrast to his own resignation. She was very sure where she was going; the shepherd's hut for her was a destination; but for him it could only be another place in which to try and solve what could never be solved.

The burn was nearly dry; to go up its bed was easy, jumping from stone to stone, screened all the time by the birches on both banks.

Then they heard shouting and whistling.

"You sit and rest," said Gillian, and waited till he obeyed.

Through the branches of a birch she gazed down at the persons gathered at the drystone dyke. Her father was there, with Alistair beside him. Two policemen were leaning against the dyke. Her mother was hurrying across the field of whins. One of the policemen took off his helmet and mopped his brow with his handkerchief. They were all troubled by midges. It was only when she saw them waving handkerchiefs about their faces that she became aware she too was being tormented.

Alistair whistled, with his fingers in his mouth; it was she who had taught him to whistle like that. Her father shouted. Among the whins her mother stopped to call; and from the tremulousness of that calling Gillian knew she must be weeping. There was no sign of any of Tom's people. Perhaps they had got away in the bus after all.

Gillian went back and crouched beside Tom. Some of her resolution was lost.

"Anyway, it's hopeless," she muttered, and bit at her knee.

He sat so still she could scarcely hear him breathe. A trickle of water, a grasshopper, a faraway curlew, Alistair whistling: these she heard, with poignant clarity, but him she could not hear at all. He might have been dead. Midges crawled up his face, and into his ears and hair, a green insect landed on his knee; but he did not move his hand to chase them away. Blood was seeping through the bandage on his other hand.

"Did you," she asked, "did you steal those things in Woolworth's because — because you didn't want — to get — too fond of us?"

Expressed like that, almost angrily as if she was again accusing him, it was very far from saying what was in her heart to say. She felt not only pity and love for him in his terrible predicament, but also complicity with him. There was no way of explaining that.

Nevertheless he seemed to understand, and smiled with a gratitude she could not bear. She leapt up.

"If we're going to get to the hut before it's too dark," she said, "we'd better hurry."

The way led through the deep narrow gorge of the burn, across a wide area of black peat-hags, and over bright green marshes. Once they passed the skull of a sheep.

"They often die in the snow," said Gillian.

At last they arrived in the hollow where the fank and hut were.

Before she untied the string that fastened the door of the hut Gillian stood listening. Shouts could still be heard. She was sure they were made by her father who was toiling up the hill after them. He knew of this hut; last year he had brought her and Alistair up here on an expedition. When he came he would advise her what to do.

The hut was very small. In it were a zinc bucket, an old newspaper, many dead flies, a piece of creosoted rope, fragments of fleece, and the broken top of a Thermos flask.

"We'll wait here," said Gillian. "You sit down." She upturned the bucket for him.

"You sit."

"No. I might not be staying. I mean, I'll have to go out and make sure Daddy doesn't miss us. It's getting dark. He's not really got a good sense of direction. So you'd better sit down."

He sat down.

She stood gazing at him. "Is your hand sore?"

He shook his head.

"It must be."

There was nothing she could think of to say. Now that she had brought him here she could not see what good it had done. It was impossible for him to stay with her family always, and it seemed to her no less impossible for him to return to Donaldson's Court with

254

his own family; there was nowhere she could advise him to go.

"I'm sorry I called you a traitor," she said. "For not speaking to Peerie, I mean."

Then she remembered his mother at the tree as he was punching it. If Mrs Curdie was *her* mother, would she be able to honour her? The question, with its dreadful but inevitable answer, brought her even closer to him, but never close enough.

"Maybe I should go out now and see where Daddy is," she said.

Suddenly the smallness, darkness, and desolation of the hut, and its uselessness as a refuge for him, overwhelmed her with terror. If she did not get out into the open at once, and see the sky, she would begin to scream and not be able to stop. Adding to her terror, too, were his patience and silence as he sat on the bucket, with his bandaged hand resting on his knee, and his face glimmering like the skull they had passed on the hill.

She pushed at the door. When it did not instantly open, her hands became as if paralysed; her strength seemed all to have gone. Even her sobbing was low and difficult.

He rose and pushed the door open with his foot.

As she rushed out, she thought the sky had never looked so beautiful and spacious.

"Will you be all right?" she cried.

She thought he answered, "Yes."

"I'll not be long. We'll have to hurry, won't we, for it's getting awfully dark?"

She clambered up out of the hollow. When she saw the beam of the lighthouse and the lights of Wemyss Bay across the Firth, she felt reassured. Two or three stars twinkled in the sky. Making an effort to be calm she put her hands to her mouth and shouted, "Daddy, Daddy, Daddy." From faraway there seemed to come an answer. She shouted again, but this time no answer came. What she had feared must have happened; making for the hut her father had wandered off in the wrong direction.

There was only one thing to do now: she and Tom would have to go down. She could scout on ahead and find out if the police were gone; but, of course, even if they were, they would come back again tomorrow. Besides, her mother and grandmother would be more angry with him than ever, because she had got herself into trouble by helping him. Her father too might be lost all night.

With a gesture of surrender she went back down into the hollow, which in these last few minutes had grown much darker.

The door was closed. Pushing it open, and calling his name, she screamed. He was a giant staring with a queer twist down at her. At first she thought he must be standing on the bucket until she remembered that the door in opening had struck it. Then she made out round his neck, in a noose, the rope which she had noticed lying on the floor. Often she had seen Alistair play thus, pretending to be a cowboy hero about to be lynched; she herself had joined in. It was the memory of those games, so lively and so happily foolish, that made this silent, lonely, melancholy imitation so terrifying.

Then she knew. The rope was not loose, it was fastened to a nail in the rafter. She screamed again and again, but stopped suddenly, and was as still as death, when he tried to gurgle something to her.

She knew if she could keep calm she might be able to save him; but that very effort at calmness exhausted her. First she held him up to take the weight off his neck; but she could not do that for long, so she dragged the pail over to her with her foot, kicked it so that it stood upside down, climbed on to it, still trying to hold him up with one hand, and with the other hand reached up and tried to untie the rope or break it or pull out the nail. All that happened was that her hand grew cramped and seared. If only she had a knife, she kept moaning; and vividly she remembered the little knife with the mother-of-pearl handle that Alistair was so proud of, and which their mother didn't like him to have. When she tried to loose the noose her fingers against his cold neck became weak as a baby's.

That was all she had the courage to try. When the pail fell, bringing her down heavily and painfully, she ran out, limping, with her leg skinned and bleeding. Again she saw the beam of the lighthouse and the lights of Wemyss Bay, much brighter now that sky and sea and hills were dark; but this time there was no reassurance in their reminder of people at peace at the fireside in their homes.

Weeping, and falling often, she made her way at a desperate pace down the hill.

Afterword

Reincarnation may be an increasingly fashionable belief in the West but Robin Jenkins was a rare man in experiencing it firsthand. A novelist whose work spanned half a century, he was effectively rediscovered and reborn as a public figure in the 1980s, thanks to a combination of new books, and the republication of some of his earlier classics. Before he died in 2005, he had become a prophet honoured in his own country and his lifetime, an unusual fate for a Scot. Like countless others, I discovered him from the paperbacks that began appearing then. There was *The Cone Gatherers,* his haunting forest novel of the Second World War, still his best-known book, but then *Fergus Lamont, Just Duffy, Dust on the Paw* and many more. A fine novelist has an atmosphere, a saturated colour, all his or her own, and Jenkins has it. It's ultimately indescribable, something to be seen or tasted, but it has something to do moral intelligence, social conscience, an acute understanding of life's absurdity and deep human sympathy.

★ ★ ★

John Jenkins (as he was known outside writing) had been brought up in a tough Lanarkshire mining village in deep poverty, before becoming a school-teacher, a wartime conscientious objector working in Argyll's forests and, for a while, a militant socialist. Yet after the collapse of his party, the Independent Labour Party, he described himself as a moralist rather than anything else, and it is the moral cutting edge of his writing that makes him a lot more directly challenging than most contemporary novelists, even if they are slicker and subtler in style. At his finest he is the Scottish Ibsen, or even Chekhov, in the intensity and dark plunge of his thinking. My favourite for a long time was an historical novel, *The Awakening of George Darroch*, about the least likely of subjects, the struggle of a Church of Scotland minister about whether to abandon his living when the Kirk split over its relationship with the early Victorian state. Jenkins took this very important but also musty-smelling issue as the background for a book about conscience, frailty and oppression that could help anyone today to understand life in Communist Eastern Europe, or indeed the agonising choices currently faced by Islamists in Pakistan and Afghanistan — a part of the world Jenkins knew well.

Then I came across *The Changeling*. It usurped even *George Darroch*, which it much resembles. The setting is nearer to us in time but yet a world away already. This is emphatically not a book which "could have been written today" and that's part of the point. It tells the story of a fat, sentimental, not very successful schoolteacher who believes in human goodness, and who tries to reclaim, or save, a bright boy from the Glasgow slums by taking him on his family holiday. That, by the way, already distances the story. Once, not so long ago, middle-class people did sometimes do things like that. The more Christian atmosphere of Scotland in the middle of the twentieth century, and the equally idealistic socialism of the time, could provoke people to reach out, as they don't today, after another half-century of rising incomes and waning faith — religious and political. Even in 1956–7, roughly the time of the novel's setting, the majority of people regard the teacher's action as naïve and possibly hypocritical (perhaps he's trying to attract attention to get a promotion). But it was less outlandish then.

Jenkins was interested in naïve people, including those trying to do good in a cold, materialist world. In *The Changeling* the teacher, Charlie Forbes, is both risible and impressive. The story depends upon him being, like most of us, a curdled mix of vanity, ambition, selfishness, sentimentality — and altruism. We are frequently reminded of his clumsy, flat-footed absurdity; on a bicycle with buckled wheels, "in mauve corduroy shorts, leather moccasins, and white open-necked shirt that revealed the hairiness of his broad chest, he sang as he zig-zagged in the sunshine . . ." He responds to the beauty of the Argyllshire landscape with unrestrained romanticism, an absurd mix of half-digested history and childish romance. He is what Scots call "a terrible blether", a humbug and a bore — as one of the other teachers tells him to his face, "smug and phoney". And indeed he is almost completely impossible. But only "almost". Though most of those around him reckon that he is a hypocrite, Forbes is more interesting than that. He has had Quixotic moments before. Once he invited a labourer to join a family picnic — almost casually we learn that eight years on, the bitter and bereaved man recalls the tea "still sweet in his mooth". Random acts of goodness ricochet and reverberate. He knows it, even if hardly anyone else seems to remember. In his galumphing, ridiculous way, Forbes retains a fundamental optimism about humanity without which we are lost souls.

So he is genuinely moved by the sharp brightness of the slum boy, Tom Curdie. Unlike the rest of the school staff, his wife, children and mother-in-law, all more cynical and worldly-wise, he doesn't see Curdie's unsettling half-smile as insolence, but as rather brave. His scheme for Curdie has a trickle of sly ambition about it but even Forbes cannot work out how much. At one level, the other teachers who are brutal, coarse and unethical are right and he is wrong. Curdie is indeed a "practised liar and a thief". He is deep and devious. Living with an alcoholic mother and a crippled stepfather in a tenement with his brother and sister, he is brutalised, veiled, armoured. In a few strokes, Jenkins draws the life of industrial poverty as deftly as Dickens, and without a flicker of sentiment. These are poor people. And partly because they are poor, they turn out to be nasty people too. Here, there is nothing redeeming about poverty. "Donaldson's Court", the slum where the Curdies live, is a place which stands in the book for the worst in modern life. The others are right to fear and shun it. In a rare example of authorial moralising, Jenkins picks up on one character's assertion that he wouldn't let a pet tiger into Donaldson's Court, bitterly agreeing that "its sleek skin, indigenous to jungle striped with sun and shadow, would have been shamed, and its fastidious paws polluted, by the garbage, filth and overflow from broken privies". Humans, however, he points out, "had begun to acquire the characteristics which would enable them to survive amidst that dirt and savagery . . . as irretrievably adapted to their environment as the tiger to his".

Yet, at a more important level, Forbes is right and his critics are wrong. Tom Curdie steals for money to help his friends, but also he steals to keep himself from going soft. The frightened, beaten-down, beautiful human being spotted by the teacher is there, hidden behind his circumstances and intelligence. Tom knows how the world goes. He brings a bite of apple to a mangy cat and strokes it: "Suspicious of kindness, it mewed in misery at being too weak to slink away. He did not speak either to reassure or sympathise. Pity was never shown by him, only comradeship." (There is a socialist undercurrent in the book as strong as in Lewis Grassic Gibbon's *Scots Quair* or the poetry of Hugh MacDiarmid but much quieter.) For Tom stealing is something protective, a palisade which will shore up the distance between him and the Forbeses. It is self-definition of a pessimistic kind. It keeps out feelings that might weaken Tom in the vicious fight for survival that is slum life. He understands that if he lets

262

himself believe that he belongs in the comfortable middle-class Forbes family, with their good food, indoor lavatories and country holidays, then when he goes back to reality, life will be intolerable.

For Tom is not being offered adoption. He is not being "saved". He is being given a tantalising glimpse of a better, brighter, more beautiful world, before it is snatched back and he is returned to a world that stinks of piss and booze and failure. This better world is embodied in the fictional Argyllshire village of Towellan, a magically beautiful seaside setting that anyone who knows the west of Scotland will instantly recognise, an apparent Arcadia which represents for the Forbes family their annual paradise. Like the Borders countryside in Hugh MacDiarmid's poetry, or Orkney in the writing of Edwin Muir, it stands for a dream of uncorrupted, pre-industrial human life, to be set against the worst of Scottish mid-century slums. For the Forbeses, "Towellan" means family harmony, unforced laughter and shared experiences as banal as favourite walks or unsuccessful fishing trips — a seam of joy to be hoarded and savoured for the rest of the year. So to take Tom Curdie with him, Forbes believes, is not a small thing. It may somehow inoculate him — with optimism, or vital human spirit. It will at least show him another way of living. That this is both well-meaning and obtuse, even cruel, is something that hard, bright Curdie instinctively grasps but his teacher, brimming with naïveté, is simply too stupid to understand. What is he about? Does he think he can save someone with a fortnight in a cottage?

So this is a moral battle, fought out by ordinary people, who rarely understand one another yet for whom time is short. Forbes, apparently risking nothing worse than a little gentle ridicule, finds himself risking and losing much more than that — in effect, his own human essence, for he becomes monstrous by the end of the story. Tom Curdie, who thinks he is well protected from love and pity, is physically destroyed because Forbes has done his (wholly well-meaning) work and shown the child the full horror of returning to his own background, while knowing that he cannot stay in Paradise either: he literally has nowhere left to go. His instinctive sense that he had to protect himself, build a wall, is shown to be bitterly accurate. Meanwhile, the more hardbitten characters around these two have risked nothing and lose nothing, yet they are shown without sympathy as lost souls clothed in modern banality. Only Forbes's daughter, Gillian, who starts by hating Tom and determining to destroy him as a spy and sneak, to get him out of the family, is transformed. If there is a scrap of hope in the book, it is her journey from selfish hard-heartedness to deep empathy, of a kind which might in future be less clumsy and self-regarding than her father's.

As the action advances, barely a word or phrase is wasted. Everything is charged with moral meaning, from the diseased rabbits deliberately infected with myxomatosis to improve farmers' profits, to the Americanisms of Forbes's son, who calls his father "Pop". In the apparently timeless Argyllshire of the late

Fifties, which was Jenkins's chosen home landscape for much of his life, the surrounding world's politics is not so far away. The Holy Loch will very soon be visited by the first US Navy Polaris submarines and protestors will be marching along the roads where Forbes on his wobbly bicycle had teetered, dreaming. (One thinks of another Scottish artist, Ian Hamilton Finlay, who died a year after Jenkins: his garden refuge or temple in the Pentland hills, Little Sparta, featured stone-carved battleships, submarines and sharks: "Et in Arcadia Ego'). In the Fifties, package holidays abroad would soon dilute the old raucous Glaswegian rituals of going "doon the watter". Pop music would kill off the open-air singing competition shown in the book — indeed, it apparently already is dead. The teachers belting and abusing slum children are themselves on the way out. So too is the old culture of Scotland generally, so sentimentally admired by Forbes. Anyone who still thinks that Britain in the Fifties was a reassuring and stable society would be well advised to read this novel attentively.

This being Jenkins at his best, all the characters are wholly human, fallible and at times ridiculous, from the middle-class mother-in-law to the drunken slum parents. Except for Tom and Gillian they appear at first as actors in a comedy, not a tragedy. Yet the world they live in is a tragic world because the possibility of transforming escape for Tom Curdie, or a universe in which Forbes is intelligent enough to think through the consequences of his actions, seems here unthinkable. Some readers may revolt against this. After all, better housing, less brutal education and the expansion of the universities did allow many people to escape, including Jenkins himself. The curt destruction of Forbes's inflated do-goodery has a sadism about it too. There is no getting away from the fact that this is a bleak little book, for all the sunlight and summer laughter. Nor is it perfect. There is a strange cat-and-mouse pursuit of the family by Peerie, Tom's friend, towards the end. Like everything else here it serves a particular function — it finally exposes cheerful Charlie Forbes — but it is ridiculous too. To this, I would only say that it is a tragedy, and tragedies may have interludes, and that there is a need for tragic insight always. This book makes me cry, and unsettles me badly, and yet I pick it up again, and press it on friends. It has settled itself somewhere inside my mind, and stayed. What more can you say?

Andrew Marr, 2007

266

Also available in ISIS Large Print:

The Nickum

Doris Davidson

Willie Fowlie's grandmother calls him a "nickum" — he is a mischievous Aberdeenshire boy who often acts instinctively, bearing little consideration for the consequences of his actions.

Willie's headmaster recognises his potential and finances his matriculation at University along with his daughter, Millie. Free from the constraints of their childhood, the blossoming of their love begins to unfold. But within weeks of the outbreak of war, Willie's oldest friend enlists in the army. Implored to sign up with him, Willie feels duty-bound to his sponsor to finish his degree and turns him down.

Two years later, news arrives announcing that his friend has been killed in action. Racked with guilt, Willie abandons his education and volunteers for the Gordon Highlanders. The course of his life is now completely changed, but can the "nickum" ever atone for the decisions that he has made?

ISBN 978-0-7531-8196-6 (hb)
ISBN 978-0-7531-8197-3 (pb)

In Zodiac Light

Robert Edric

December 1922. Ex-soldier, poet and composer Ivor Gurney, suffering from increasingly frequent and deepening bouts of paranoid schizophrenia, is transferred to the City of London Mental Hospital, Dartford. Neglected by all but a notable handful of his friends, Gurney begins a descent into madness and oblivion. Yet there are those who continue to believe in Gurney's capabilities — in his "wayward genius".

Few of those now responsible for Gurney realise the consequences of their hopefulness. They have no real idea of what he had endured on the Western Front and the effects it had on his mind. Ultimately it is not the war but the refusal of his admirers to acknowledge the trauma of his experience that will take him further from a creative rebirth and closer to the edge of sanity that he both craves and fears . . .

ISBN 978-0-7531-8244-4 (hb)
ISBN 978-0-7531-8245-1 (pb)